PENGUIN BOOKS

REILLY: THE FIRST MAN

Robin Bruce Lockhart is the author of *Reilly: Ace of
Spies* (Penguin), which appeared on PBS in a very pop-
ular Mobil "Mystery!" series presentation. He is a former
newspaper executive who was foreign manager of *The
Financial Times* (London). He was educated in France,
Switzerland, Germany, and the Royal Naval College,
Dartmouth, before going to Cambridge University. His
father, Sir Robert Bruce Lockhart, was head of the
English mission in Moscow and worked extensively
with Sidney Reilly. Mr. Bruce Lockhart lives in Sussex,
England.

REILLY:
THE FIRST MAN

Robin Bruce Lockhart

PENGUIN BOOKS

PENGUIN BOOKS
Viking Penguin Inc., 40 West 23rd Street,
New York, New York 10010, U.S.A.
Penguin Books Ltd, Harmondsworth,
Middlesex, England
Penguin Books Australia Ltd, Ringwood,
Victoria, Australia
Penguin Books Canada Limited, 2801 John Street,
Markham, Ontario, Canada L3R 1B4
Penguin Books (N.Z.) Ltd, 182–190 Wairau Road,
Auckland 10, New Zealand

First published in Penguin Books 1987
Published simultaneously in Canada

LIBRARY OF CONGRESS CATALOGING IN PUBLICATION DATA
Lockhart, Robin Bruce.
Reilly : the first man.
1. Reilly, Sidney George, 1874–1925. 2. Spies—
Great Britain—Biography. I. Title.
UB271.G72R4542 1984   327.1'2'0924 [B]   86-25600
ISBN 0 14 01.0027 X

Printed in The United States of America by
Offset Paperback Mfrs., Inc., Dallas, Pennsylvania
Set in Times Roman

This book is dedicated to all those engaged in the unseen and ceaseless intelligence war on behalf of the United States and her allies. Their work helps to preserve peace more than the general public realizes.

Contents

Contents

Preface

Hundreds of thousands of people have now read my book *Reilly: Ace of Spies*, and millions more, the world over, have seen the popular television series based on it. For a full appreciation of *Reilly: The First Man* it is essential that those who have not read my first book on Sidney Reilly, or have learned about him only from their television screens, should have a broad picture of the real truth about the master-spy who dominated the espionage world from the turn of the century until he "disappeared" into Russia in 1925 in highly unusual circumstances. What became of him is a mystery to this day. In the final episode of the television series, Reilly is seen being executed by a firing squad: This is roughly in line with one of the many contradictory stories about Reilly put out by the Russians in unofficial accounts. The Soviets have never issued any official statement about him at all.

As I wrote in the last paragraph of the last chapter of *Reilly: Ace of Spies*:

The fate of Sigmund Rosenblum,* the bastard of Odessa, who emerged from the jungles of Brazil to become Britain's master spy, is probably destined to be forever shrouded in mist.

*Sidney Reilly's real name.

Whereas the television producers wanted a "tidy" ending for the series, I argued strenuously—to no avail—that the series ought to have ended with the truth in so far as it was known: i.e., that what ultimately became of Reilly is a complete mystery. There is no concrete proof of his death. For many years I strived to solve the mystery, and not long ago I lighted on startling new evidence unearthed from among my father's papers that indicated that Reilly lived on well after his "disappearance" in 1925. The results of my subsequent research were corroborative and the dramatic consequences are the subject of this book.

In Chapter I, for the benefit of those who have not read *Reilly: Ace of Spies*, I give a brief résumé of the master-spy's career; but the reader should also know something of the reputation he had earned for himself during his lifetime. Today, the activities of those working in the intelligence world are the subject of almost daily reports or comments in the Western press. Whether they are employed by the KGB or are operatives of a NATO power, they are but cogs in the vast complex machines that are the norm in modern intelligence gathering.

Sidney Reilly was of quite a different caliber from today's secret agent. An individualist par excellence, he achieved spectacular espionage feats single-handed. His disappearance into Russia in 1925 hit the headlines in the world press, with the notable exception of Russia's. Newspapers acclaimed him as "the greatest spy in history," "one of the most amazing men of his generation," "almost incredible," "no more amazing story has ever been told."

Reilly was known to all the major intelligence services of the world, yet none—not even the British Secret Service who were his principal employers—were quite sure of his origins or even of his real name. He spoke seven languages and was said to have had eleven wives and a passport to go with each. Certainly his charisma was legendary and, although one cannot be sure how many of his numerous lady friends went through a form of marriage with him, and how many were mistresses, I did discover that he had committed bigamy on at least two occasions—once with the full knowledge of the British Secret Service chief, who even attended the wedding ceremony.

One of Reilly's wives, the South American actress Pepita Bobadilla, published a melodramatic book in 1931 entitled *The Adventures of Sidney Reilly—Britain's Master Spy*. Ghosted by a journalist, the book covered but a brief part of Reilly's life and, at the time, the *Daily Mail* of London aptly commented: "Whether it is all fact and contains no fiction may be questioned by those who knew him well." And yet my father, the late Sir Robert Bruce Lockhart, whose name was bracketed with Reilly's in what the Soviets still term "The Lockhart Plot" to assassinate Lenin, and who knew Reilly well, wrote: "There are episodes in Reilly's life which are more astonishing than those recounted in this book."

Although I myself had only seen Reilly when I was a boy in Prague, for many years the mystery of his life and eventual disappearance posed a conundrum I was determined to try to solve one day. It was a mystery, I must point out, the solution to which had eluded the secret services of the world—except perhaps that of the Soviet Union.

Despite various unofficial and contradictory Russian stories about Reilly, from the date of his disappearance in 1925 until now, the Soviets have never issued any official statement about him.

It was in the mid-1960s that I decided eventually to make serious efforts to unravel the tangled tale of Sidney Reilly. I was fortunate in that a number of those who had known and worked with Reilly were still alive and, thankfully, felt sufficiently distanced in time from the events to ignore the restrictions of the British Official Secrets Act. The result was my book *Ace of Spies*, the true life story, such as it was possible to reconstruct, of a man of seemingly epic heroism and whom my father described as having been "cast in the Napoleonic mould."

Nevertheless, readers should know that there were those in the intelligence community who considered Reilly to be an adventurous scoundrel who had probably ultimately thrown in his lot with the Soviets to save his skin. Much more to the point were the views of some of the hierarchy in M15, Britain's counter-intelligence service, in particular those of M15's leading "mole" hunter, who believed that Reilly was "The First Man"—to use his own words to me at the time—to have defected. There was abundant circumstantial evidence to show that it was Reilly who had paved the way for Burgess, Maclean, Philby, Blunt, et al.

While not accepting this top mole hunter's theory in its entirety, the new evidence I have unearthed has forced me to reconsider the whole question of what became of Reilly following his disappearance in 1925. Factual evidence apart, as in crime detection, circumstantial evidence can sometimes lead to a better reconstruction of a crime than that obtained from eyewitness accounts. This holds equally true in the world of intelligence. This, then, is the story of Reilly since his return to Russia, in accordance with the facts and circumstantial evidence; and where I have found gaps, I have drawn logical inferences. *Reilly: The First Man* also delineates the roles of several of the principal "tools" deployed by the Soviets in what I call "The Reilly Gambit," to establish and maintain their continuing penetration of the West.

Many people helped make this book possible but, where they are past or present members of the United States or British intelligence communities or other governmental departments, they have generally insisted on complete anonymity. For their assistance and guidance I am deeply grateful.

In the case of information from Russian sources, wittingly or unwittingly helpful, I have in general withheld their names, also, lest they or their families suffer in any way.

On the other hand, I regret that the laws of copyright have prevented me from publishing some important correspondence from among my father's papers and that in several cases, where people are still alive and known to have been active Soviet agents, as the laws of libel frequently prevent even the truth from being published, I have had to keep some additional information in cold storage for the time being.

REILLY:
THE FIRST MAN

CHAPTER I

Window on the Past

One day, in the hot Moscow summer of 1918, a group of men assembled in a dingy basement flat. Among them was Dmitrievich Kalamatiano, an American of Greco-Russian origins who was head of U.S. Secret Intelligence in Russia. Also present were Colonel Henri de Vertement, head of the French Secret Service, and other agents of the Western Allies. Britain's master-spy, Sidney Reilly, chaired the meeting. The *i*'s were being dotted and the *t*'s being crossed to Reilly's intricate plan to overthrow Lenin and his Bolshevik henchmen who had seized power in Russia.

Reilly had subverted the Latvian mercenary guards who protected the Bolshevik leaders and had recruited a new provisional government, which he himself would orchestrate. The plan that the world has come to know as "The Lockhart Plot," because of the close links between Reilly and my father, who was Lloyd George's special envoy to the Bolsheviks, really should have been called "The Reilly Plot."

Yet, in the immortal words of Robert Burns: "The best made plans o' mice an' men gang aft a-gley." On August 31st, 1918, Dora Kaplan, an ardent Social-Revolutionary who was not connected with Reilly in any way, made an attempt on Lenin's life that only wounded him. Feliks Dzerzhinsky, head of the dreaded Cheka,[1] and his murderous gangs went into action. The Red Terror had begun: thousands of possible enemies of the Bolsheviks were shot. The *Cheka Bulletin* howled for blood: "Let there be floods of blood of the bourgeois—more blood, as much as possible."

At the same time, the Reilly plot was betrayed by one Réné Marchand, the Moscow correspondent of the French newspaper *Figaro*, a Communist sympathizer whom de Vertement had rashly taken into his confidence.

Of the plotters, Reilly, George Hill—another British agent—de Vertement, Boris Savinkov, the leading Social-Revolutionary, and others escaped.

Many were caught, tried and executed.[2] My father was arrested and thrown into the Kremlin. Expecting execution daily, he was eventually exchanged for Maxim Litvinov, the Bolshevik representative in London, whom the British had arrested in a reprisal move.

Who was this man Reilly who so nearly changed twentieth-century history? According to Reilly himself—information checked as far as possible by his Secret Service colleagues—he was born in or near Odessa[3] on March 24th, 1874, the illegitimate son of a Tsarist colonel's wife and her lover, a Jewish doctor named Rosenblum. Learning of his true parentage, the teenage Sigmund Rosenblum quit Russia and stowed away on board a merchant ship bound for Brazil, where for three years he worked as a docker, as a cook on the road, and even as a doorman at a brothel.

In 1895, three officers of British Military Intelligence exploring the Amazon engaged the young Sigmund as cook, but were struck by his expert marksmanship with a revolver when beating off an attack by hostile natives. They were also much impressed by his fluency in several languages. He was persuaded to return with them to Britain where a career in Intelligence was assured.

Soon after his arrival in England and a brief "trial" espionage mission to Russia, and an equally brief but hectic love affair with the young Ethel Voynich (author of *The*

Gadfly), he married one Margaret Thomas, a wealthy young widow, and changed his name to Sidney Reilly—Reilly being Margaret's maiden name. Many suspected that Reilly, among whose many attributes was a knowledge of medicines, hastened the end of Margaret's elderly husband. Sidney Reilly, master-spy, was born.

From then on Reilly's spying career began in earnest. In Holland, during the Boer War, he reported on British arms shipments to South Africa. Soon afterward he was in Persia. The Royal Navy's chiefs aspired to convert ships from coal-burning vessels to warships using a new wonder—fuel oil— and Reilly was sent to Persia where the Shah had given an Australian, William Knox D'Arcy, the sole concession rights of oil exploration. In addition to Britain, Russia and France had their eyes on the oil fields. Reilly's talents for intrigue and disguise and his unquestionable charm enabled him, at the eleventh hour, to obtain the Persian oil concession for Britain. Disguised as a priest, he gate-crashed a meeting at which D'Arcy was just about to sign an agreement with the French. With a sob story about an orphanage charity, he lured D'Arcy away to sign with Britain. Thus was born the Anglo-Persian Oil Company, later to become known to millions throughout the world as the British Petroleum Co. Ltd., or more simply B.P.

There followed an assignment in the Far East, in the Liaotung Peninsula of China, where the Russians were rapidly fortifying a base at Port Arthur in anticipation of the Russian-Japanese war, which broke out in February 1904.

Reilly suborned a dockyard draughtsman and photographed for transmission to Britain plans of all the defenses. He also sent back to Britain his wife, Margaret, who had become an alcoholic.

Information given to me recently by the British author Richard Deacon[4] indicates that at this time Reilly decided to play the dangerous game of double agent—triple agent, in fact—supplying intelligence not only to Britain but to Japan and to Russia as well. Deacon had been told the whole

story by the late Richard Hughes, formerly Tokyo correspondent of *The Times* (London) and *The Financial Times*.
Hughes was a highly responsible journalist who knew Japan
intimately and who had developed a curiosity about intelligence operations in Japan since the mid-nineteenth century.
He had also come to know the brilliant Soviet agent Sorge,[5]
known as "The Man with Five Faces" and had been close
to Ian Fleming, personal assistant to the British director of
naval Intelligence in World War II.

According to Hughes, Colonel Motojiro Akashi,[6] Chief
of Staff of the Japanese forces in Korea at the turn of the
century, inveigled Reilly into working for the Japanese. The
two men had met earlier in St. Petersburg, which Akashi
had visited periodically not only as a roving European attaché, but also as an agent of the Black Dragon secret
society. Reilly, whose equivocal activities in Port Arthur
had aroused the suspicions of the Okhrana, which mistak-
enly believed he was working only for them, welcomed
Akashi's invitation to work for him in Tokyo for, apparently,
a handsome cash payment.

It is not clear how long Reilly spent in Tokyo, but it was
long enough, again according to Hughes, for Reilly to become involved in another hectic love affair with an Englishwoman by the name of Anne Luke. At the same time, there
was a curious murder case in Japan in which another
Englishwoman, Elizabeth Carew, was sentenced to death
by a British consular court for poisoning her husband Walter.
There were strong suspicions that the one who had really
committed the murder was Reilly's mistress, Anne Luke,
and Mrs. Carew's sentence was commuted to life imprisonment.

Despite extensive investigations, Richard Hughes could
reach no final conclusions on the Carew-Luke-Reilly tri-
angle or quadrangle, but the manner of the elimination of
Walter Carew reminds one uncannily of the demise of Margaret's first husband, the Reverend Hugh Thomas.

It is doubtful if Reilly stayed very long in Japan or that

he gave the Japanese much information about Russian defenses in Port Arthur. Hughes was of the opinion that Reilly
was attracted by the money offered and had very probably
already become involved with Anne Luke, another reason
why he wanted Margaret to leave the Far East.

This whole episode, revealing Reilly as a double agent,
is important circumstantial evidence that has to be taken
into account in any reappraisal of his later loyalties—or
disloyalties.

On his return to London, Reilly found that Margaret had
withdrawn all funds in their joint bank account and had
vanished without trace. His anger was, perforce, sublimated
on his next more important mission, which was to Germany.

The clouds of World War I were gathering over Europe
and, after some training in Sheffield, Reilly went to Germany in 1909 to work as a welder in the giant Krupp ar-
mament works: His mission was to obtain full details of all
the latest German armaments. Security round the drawing
office was too tight to enable him to photograph plans, but
Reilly solved the problem by volunteering for the works'
fire brigade. This involved night-shift work when security
was looser. After strangling the foreman of the night guards
and binding and gagging another guard, Reilly broke into
the drawing office one night, stole the plans, and escaped
with them to London before the hue and cry was raised.

After his adventures at Krupp, Reilly was sent once more
to Russia—to collect, through Russian sources, all the information he could get on German military and naval power
now that war was becoming increasingly probable.

On arrival in St. Petersburg, Reilly had no firm ideas
other than to organize an international air race restricted to
Russian aviators. With the help of some old friends, money
won at the gaming tables, and his persuasive charm the air
race, by stages from St. Petersburg to Moscow, was a great
success and enabled Reilly to build up connections in court

and government circles. He was now ready for a major espionage feat.

The Russian Navy destroyed in the Russian-Japanese War had to be rebuilt. The German shipyards, through their influence with the Tsar and their extensive business connections in Russia, were likely to get the contracts. In a brilliantly devised scheme, Reilly cultivated and became close friends with Massino, the naval assistant to the minister of Marine, and his attractive wife, Nadine. At the same time, he joined a relatively small company, Mendrochovich and Lubensky, which was selling Russian railway wagons to Germany. Learning from Massino that the giant naval constructors of Hamburg, Blohm, and Voss, were likely to get the contracts, he persuaded Massino to influence Blohm and Voss to appoint Mendrochovich and Lubensky as their St. Petersburg agents. This resulted in the Blohm and Voss warship designs, right down to the smallest details and very similar to those drawn up for the Kaiser's fleet, passing through the hands of Mendrochovich and Lubensky. All were photographed by Reilly and sent to London. The British firm of Vickers, which had hoped for the contracts, was furious; but the British Admiralty was delighted. In the process, Reilly earned a fat commission for himself, as well.

This success was not achieved without major problems arising in Reilly's private life. He had fallen in love with Nadine Massino, but news had reached Margaret of the upturn in Reilly's finances, and she turned up in Moscow out of the blue. Reilly was furious, but solved the problem by threatening to kill Margaret, and she fled the country. After placing a false news item in the Russian press about a railway accident in which several people had been killed, including Mrs. Reilly, he paid a considerable sum to Massino to agree to a divorce so that he could marry Nadine.

When the 1914—1918 War broke out, Reilly temporarily deserted the British Secret Service, infuriating its chief, Captain Mansfield Cumming CB, RN. The highly individualistic spy was busy first in Japan and then in the United States buying armaments on behalf of the Russian government.

In New York, in 1916, he went through a bigamous marriage with Nadine, who had come over from Europe, but in the same year he decided to rejoin the British Secret Service (then known as MI1C). For the next eighteen months Reilly accomplished numerous amazing espionage exploits, being dropped by plane many times behind the German lines. He spoke German like a native and for a short period enlisted in the German Army, being commissioned as an officer. In the most daring exploit of all, Reilly disguised himself as the chief of staff of Prince Ruprecht of Bavaria and attended a conference of the German Imperial High Command presided over by the Kaiser!

But with the Bolshevik revolution a fait accompli and with the danger that Russia might make a separate peace with Germany, Lloyd George wanted "action" from Cumming. The upshot was the dispatch of Reilly to Russia and the plot that failed, but from which Reilly returned to London with the reputation that he above all others was the man to bring down the Bolsheviks.

Apart from a brief incursion on a spying mission to southern Russia in 1919 along with his MI1C[7] colleague George Hill, from then until his "disappearance" in 1925, Reilly was mainly engaged in soliciting British, American, and French support, both practical and financial, for the anti-Bolsheviks outside Russia who were rallying to the flag of Boris Savinkov, former minister of War in the Kerensky government and leader of the Social-Revolutionaries. Reilly did not align himself with Tsarist elements among the exiles.

During the 1920s, an organization called the Moscow Municipal Credit Association was formed. More commonly known as "The Trust," it was seemingly an anti-Soviet underground movement to which many well-placed officials and officers of the Soviet government and armed forces belonged. Their emissaries moved freely in and out of Russia to make contact with Reilly, Savinkov[8]—whose cause no less a person than Winston Churchill had espoused—and their friends in France, Poland, and elsewhere. They planned a counter-revolution and invited them to Russia to confer with the leaders of "The Trust."

On August 10th, 1924, Savinkov, his aide Dehrenthal and the latter's wife, together with two messengers from "The Trust," although aware of the likelihood that "The Trust" had been penetrated by agents-provocateurs, entered Russia via Finland. Nineteen days later there was a brief report in *Pravda* that Savinkov had been arrested. Further announcements followed rapidly: he had been condemned to death; sentence had been commuted to ten years imprisonment; he had been completely acquitted and was a free man.

The GPU[9] had not been idle. "The Trust," although peppered with true anti-Bolsheviks to give it a "genuine" facade, was controlled in reality by the KRO,[10] the GPU's counter-intelligence, and was the brainchild of Artuzov, it's chief.

Savinkov was "allowed" to write a long letter[11] to Reilly from the Lubianka prison. How much of this represented his real feelings, how much was written under pressure from his jailers, and how much was pure forgery, is uncertain. The GPU, just as the KGB[12] today, was expert in producing documents which were a mixture of truth and falsehood. There is a rare book, published in Russia in 1926, purporting to be the "Last Letters of Savinkov." True or false? Once again, the answer is probably a combination of the two.

Eventually, it was reported that Savinkov had committed suicide in May 1925, by jumping out of his prison window. But was it suicide? Or was he pushed?[13] Or, as some believe, was he only killed off "on paper"? Did he live on to assist the Soviets? To add to the mystery of Savinkov, a letter from him to Marshal Pilsudski[14] dated December 29th, 1921, which has only very recently come to light, reveals that Savinkov had been having secret discussions with the Bolsheviks as early as 1921 and strongly suggests that he switched his loyalties and secretly became a Soviet agent at that time. Was Reilly aware of this?

To the world at large, Reilly proclaimed that Savinkov was a traitor and that he never should have been taken in by "The Trust" which, quite clearly, was riddled with GPU agents-provocateurs.

Yet a few months later, in September 1925, Reilly himself, aided and abetted by the British Secret Service, let it be said, crossed the Finnish border into Russia and made his way to Moscow with the stated purpose of meeting the leaders of "The Trust" and the "Shadow Cabinet" of a future non-Bolshevik Russian Government. Why did he do this, when even to a most mediocre intelligence operator, all the evidence pointed unerringly to a GPU plot? How was it possible that superspy Reilly could fall for such a ploy?

The fact is, apart from a postcard from Moscow to his third and also bigamously married wife, Pepita—although Reilly was divorced from Nadine, Margaret was still alive—not a word was heard from Reilly again.

The Russians have never, either then or since, issued any official statement about him; and the Foreign Office, as was to be expected, disclaimed any official connection with him.

However, various unofficial Russian reports in newspapers, magazines, and books, gave a variety of dates and places between 1925 and 1927 when Reilly was allegedly arrested and later tried and executed. All were contradictory accounts, as were Reilly's so-called confessions extraordinarily inaccurate when referring to his past.

Reports, true or false, that Reilly was alive and well and had been sighted in various places persisted throughout the late 1920s and the 1930s and, as already recounted, into World War II. Much of this speculation is typical of dezinformatsia[15] techniques designed to confuse the West and hide the truth—that Reilly was now the GPU's, and later the NKVD's,[16] "Number One Secret Weapon" against the Western democracies. But that the GPU should "kill" him in the media several times over on several different dates also indicates that the Soviets were worried that first reports of his "death" had not been believed.

What *is* certain is that following Reilly's disappearance, Russia's main intelligence and political strategy changed. Dzerzhinsky and his successors may have been the captains of the ship, but everything points to the hand of the navigator on the tiller frequently being that of Reilly.

CHAPTER II

Back-track

The term "Bolshevism" has been applied so promiscuously that for the purpose of this letter, I find it expedient
to define more clearly the sense in which I am using it.

I believe that in-so-far as this system contains practical
and constructive ideas for the establishment of a high
social justice, it is bound by a process of evolution to
conquer the world, as Christianity and the ideas of the
French Revolution have done before it, and that nothing—least of all violent reactionary forces—can stem
its ever-rising tide. Incidentally I should also like to state
here, that the much decried little understood "Soviets"
which are the outward expression of Bolshevism as applied to practical government, are the nearest approach,
I know of, to a *real* democracy based upon true social
justice and that they may be destined to lead the world
to the highest ideal of statesmanship—Internationalism.

So wrote Lenin? Gorki? Some other leading Russian?
No. This panegyric of Bolshevism and the Soviet system
comes straight from a letter (Appendix 1) written to my
father by none other than Sidney Reilly, before he "disappeared" into Russia. A letter discovered only after I had
completed my biography of Reilly following the death of
my father, whose papers took a long time to peruse.[1]
I have always stressed the point that the mystery of what

became of Reilly has never been solved. All Russian versions have varied and are contradictory.[2] Here was evidence that Reilly had paved the way for Philby, Burgess, and Maclean, which I had so vehemently pooh-pooed when I was questioned in the late 1960s by MI5's leading "mole hunter," could well be correct. Here was corroboration of his opinion that Reilly—and *not* one of the Cambridge moles—had been "The First Man."

Also subsequent to writing *Reilly: Ace of Spies*, I came across evidence that Baroness Moura Budberg had sent news to my father in March 1932 from Estonia that Reilly was still alive. Moura Budberg, an enigmatic but highly intelligent woman at home in high political circles of all persuasions, had been in turn my father's mistress in Russia before becoming that of Gorki and later H. G. Wells. As a result of her intimate association with Gorki, she came close to Stalin and, I have every reason to believe, met with Reilly in Russia in the late 1920s.

When Brigadier George Hill was in Moscow in World War II as liaison officer to the NKVD, his closest Russian colleague, NKVD Major Ossipov, told him that Reilly was still alive but "unwell"; he would say no more. At the time, Hill was not sure that Ossipov was telling the truth, and did not report this conversation to me, except in an oblique manner, until after *Ace of Spies* was published.

The Russians are nothing if not experts in *dezinformatsia* and in spreading confusion. It can suit them at times to "execute" people while in reality they keep them alive, and vice versa. At other times, people in the espionage world disappear without a word. This has happened to many trained CIA agents of Russian origin sent to the Soviet Union. Have they been captured and shot, "turned," or perhaps held for possible "spy-swap" occasions? No one can be sure. When Kim Philby dies, will he be given a state funeral or, to keep us all guessing, will the Soviets keep up a pretense that he is alive for the subsequent ten years or more?

As for cataloguing all the help Reilly gave the Soviets,

the full details must inevitably be speculative to some extent. Nevertheless the overall pattern is quite clear, as are the identities and activities of the main "pieces" in the Russian game of chess with the West in which the "Reilly Gambit" was the key move. The legacy he left has led eventually to major penetration at all levels of Western Intelligence communities.

One of the problems in filling in details of Reilly's post–1925 career lies in the fact that the Russian secret police records, be they those of the Cheka, NKVD, MGB, or KGB, have almost certainly been destroyed, just as most of the chiefs of the Russian secret police and their closest colleagues have been eliminated by their successors. Stalin himself was responsible for the destruction of massive quantities of records. There has been so much falsification and destruction of Cheka/GPU/NKVD records that it is very doubtful that anyone in Russia today knows very much about operations of fifty to sixty years ago.

Melor Sturua,[3] one time *Izvestia* correspondent in London and later in Washington, and as clever a KGB man as they come, once told me that there were no longer any official records in Moscow about Reilly: they had all been "lost or destroyed."

Even as late as 1981, Ernst Henri—whose real name is Simeyon Rostovsky—and who operated for the NKVD in England from 1933 until 1951, was writing in Moscow of Reilly: "Much of his biography remains unexplained."[4] The reader will learn more of Henri/Rostovsky, a key figure in NKVD/KGB activities, in later chapters.

There is in existence a *samizdat* (*a Russian underground publication*), of which I have a copy, called "My Search for Reilly the Spy",[5] by Revolt Pimenov, a leading figure in Russian academic circles who, like myself, had been struck by the extraordinary inconsistencies in Russian accounts of the Reilly story.

After carefully studying all the available documentation,

including the numerous books by Nikulin and Minaev on
Soviet espionage and counter-espionage,[6] Pimenov concluded that Reilly was none other than a super double-agent
and one of the great heroes of Russian Intelligence. He even
suggested that the Soviets erect a statue of him.

Pimenov was arrested in July 1970 and a *samizdat* report
of his trial exists in which he admits his authorship:

Prosecutor: Who typed your article "How I searched for
              Reilly the Spy" for you and to whom did you
              give it?
Pimenov: I typed the various drafts myself and my mother
              typed the fair copy. I sent it to the magazines
              History of the U.S.S.R., *Novy Mir*, and *Pros-
              tov*. I cannot remember the names of the per-
              sons to whom I gave it but I might have handed
              it to guests at home and told them the subject.

In his research, Pimenov gained access to articles in *Po-
granichnik* in 1965 and 1967—a restricted publication and
very difficult to obtain unless one had contacts in the KGB
Frontier Guard Service. Pimenov tells how Toivo Vjahi, the
Frontier Guard who helped Reilly into Russia from Finland
in 1925, was subsequently "disgraced" and "executed"—
conveniently so that he could assume another identity. He
reappeared forty years later as KGB Colonel I. M. Petrov!

Pimenov also considers Reilly's anti-Bolshevik work to
have been on a par with Philby's prewar pro-German activities as a "cover." The parallel is well drawn.

Pimenov was sentenced to exile to Syktyvkar in the far
North of Russia, where he remains to this day. The only
outsider allowed in to attend Pimenov's trial was Sakharov,
later himself sentenced to exile in Gorki.

I do not believe that Reilly was a double agent, working for
the Soviets from the early days of the Revolution and, as some
American "experts" would even have us believe, that the so-
called Lockhart Plot[7] was an agent-provocateur operation set

up by Dzerzhinsky, the head of the Cheka, together with Reilly.
Yet, I am now in total agreement with the MI5 "mole" hunter,
with whom I discussed the Reilly problem once more in 1985,
that Reilly was "turned." Even if he is not free to reveal all
the evidence, this former operative is quite dogmatic about
this; he also believes there were others working for our intelligence services of the same vintage as Reilly who were
"turned" as well. He has examined in detail the MI6 records
of the time and up to the years of the Cambridge "moles." He
said to me: "To put it crudely, the records stank, and you can
quote me as saying that."

It is not precisely clear at what point Reilly was "turned"
by the Bolsheviks; probably just before or after Savinkov's
return to Russia. Despite the ostensible evidence to the
contrary, it may be that Reilly secretly connived with "The
Trust" to bring about Savinkov's return to Russia.

What *is* clear is that the curiously contradictory Russian
stories as to the manner, place, and date of Reilly's "capture"
and "execution," and the various subsequent reports of his
reappearance, become more and more consistent when
weighed alongside Reilly's eulogy of Bolshevism and the
view of the MI5 "mole" hunter and others in the intelligence
world that Reilly was never executed by the Russians at all.
On the contrary, the world's—until then—greatest spy allied himself with Dzerzhinsky, the Bolshevik secret police
chief, and his successors to become one of the principal
architects of Soviet penetration of Western intelligence, diplomatic, political, and "establishment" communities: the
creator of "agents-of-influence." It must be borne in mind
that Reilly had always declared Russia to be his first love
and that, politically, he had always been basically to the
Left.

Quite recently I received an invitation delivered through
"underground" channels to visit Russia to meet a Soviet
citizen who was in a position to provide confirmatory evidence that Reilly lived on to carry out important espionage

work for the USSR. It was an invitation that I would have accepted most gladly except that I had reason to believe I would not be granted a visa, and that even were one granted, such a meeting would be dangerous for both of us.

In general, the U.S. intelligence agencies and American academics of the Soviet scene tend to pay considerably more attention than do their British counterparts to the study and analysis of Soviet espionage and subversion since the early days of Bolshevism. Despite the multitude of technical aids available to today's intelligence services, such study has revealed notable connecting themes in Soviet espionage thinking—both in terms of strategy and tactics. New enigmatic activities can often be solved and future Soviet activities forecast by interpretive analyses of even vaguely similar situations that have arisen in the past. Deviations from the Soviet espionage norm ring alarm bells.

At the time of Reilly's return to Russia, the CIA and its team of backroom historical analysts had not been created. Views about Reilly in American intelligence circles are mixed. Some believe, as I do, that he lived on well after 1925; others think he was executed. I do not. Some maintain he had been a Russian agent from the outset of his career, which I do not agree with, either. What is clear, however, is that a major deviation from what I have termed "the Soviet espionage norm" occurred following Reilly's return to the Soviet Union—a deviation that changed GPU/NKVD/KGB strategy for years to come.

No author should be afraid to back-track on what he has previously written when new information on his subject comes to light. Readers of *Reilly: Ace of Spies* who have come to look on Reilly as an anti-communist hero have no real right to condemn him as a traitor. Russian-born and bred, with Jewish blood—like Lenin[8] himself—and an espionage professional to his fingertips, he was torn between conflicting loyalties, and I believe it was his mother country which claimed his later years.

CHAPTER III

Wanderer's Return

A combination of factors was responsible for Reilly's decision in late 1924 or, more probably, in early 1925 to return to the Soviet fold—not in counter-revolutionary guise but to help, in his own way, in the building of the new Russia.

In the fall of 1924, Reilly's finances were at a low ebb, and since May 1923, he had had the added burden of his new wife, Pepita. In an attempt to restock his resources, with money borrowed to pay the fare, Reilly crossed the Atlantic to bring a lawsuit in New York against the Baldwin Locomotive Company for commission allegedly due to him in respect of war supplies purchased for the Tsarist Government. He lost the case on a technicality and his faith in justice in a capitalist society was crushed.

Upon his return to Britain, Reilly realized that the British Secret Service was toying with him, encouraging him to visit Russia to meet the leaders of the so-called Trust, the underground anti-Bolshevik resistance movement, although Reilly was well aware that the "Trust" was in reality a GPU agent-provocateur operation. Moreover, Reilly was convinced that Rear Admiral Hugh Sinclair, the SIS chief, and his closest colleagues were highly suspicious of the "Trust" and only wished to use Reilly to find out whether or not their suspicions were true. With the return of Savinkov to Russia, Reilly reasoned that the British, realizing that there was no longer any rallying point for any serious counter-revolutionary movement, were hoping that he just might turn up something in Russia in the way of a trump card: if not, he was now a spent force. Reilly had never been able to establish the same sort of relationship with Sinclair that he had had with his predecessor Cumming;[1] and he had no intention of being treated as "expendable."

Clearly, Reilly had thought long and hard about the letter (Appendix II) that Savinkov had written him from Moscow in October. Doubtless he had read the letter a number of times seeking some confirmation that his initial rage at what he considered to be Savinkov's treachery in returning to Moscow to do a deal with the Soviets had been misplaced. After all, politically the Social-Revolutionaries were not very far apart from the Communists. The enmity between them related more to power and personalities than anything else. All his life, a socialist by instinct and inclination, but admittedly a lover of power and intrigue, Reilly wondered if he had nailed his flag to the wrong mast in allying himself with Savinkov. The British and his own penchant for dramatic deeds more than anything else had led him in the first instance into derring-do in 1918 against his mother country, Russia—in so far as he had a mother country at all.

For weeks Reilly must have wrestled with his increasingly adaptable conscience, trying to reconcile his various loyalties and to work out the implications of a return to Russia. He would have to forge a fool-proof deal with Dzerzhinsky and the GPU that would guarantee his safety. At the same time he would not want his British friends and his wife Pepita to consider him a traitor.

When Reilly reached his decision to return to Russia, if he were not to be considered a traitor, he would have to "disappear" for good. And, the only way to make a lasting disappearance would be to "die." Reilly had already faked his "death" in Odessa as a young man; it is logical that his mind now turned once again to the idea of a staged "death." Such a "death," were it at the hands of the GPU, would not only leave his reputation in Britain untarnished, but would

provide a first-class cover to enable Reilly, with an assumed
identity, to build a new life and career in Russia. He would
become one of the most potent of weapons in the GPU's
armory.

The success of the plan would depend on the least number
of people knowing. No one in England—not even Pepita,
alas, as she could never hold her tongue. And in Russia
also—the fewer the better. Indeed, the majority of the GPU
hierarchy would have to be enjoined to crow over the "death"
of Reilly, and *Pravda* encouraged to extol the GPU's
achievement in eliminating him. His cover would be complete. But how to get word to Dzerzhinsky? There were a
number of known GPU agents who operated against émigrés
in the Baltic states, especially in Finland, but he knew none
personally. Undoubtedly Boris Bunakov, the SIS man in
Helsinki, would know some GPU operatives by name, but
he could hardly approach Bunakov without questions being
asked and, in any event, there was no way of ensuring the
reliability of anyone Bunakov might name.

How Reilly made his approach to Dzerzhinsky is not
clear, nor is it clear whether Melor Sturua was telling me
the truth when he told me that all relevant records of the
period had been lost or destroyed. In all probability he
adopted the simplest method of approach and asked the
Russian chargé d'affaires in London (Christov Roskovsky),
to forward by diplomatic bag a letter to Dzerzhinsky offering
his services to Russia and to the GPU in particular. Russia
was his mother country, he had always been a Socialist at
heart, he was disillusioned with capitalist society. He believed that Communism would triumph over the world in
the long run.

Reilly had much to offer Russia and the GPU; no one in
Russia knew the intelligence services of the capitalist countries as well as he did. He did not know whether Savinkov
was alive or dead, but he knew that the Savinkov cause was
dead. He was ready to return to Russia if Dzerzhinsky gave

him his word that his life would not be endangered and that
there should be no publicity to the effect that he had defected
from Britain. On the contrary, he could be of greatest service
to Russia if the world were to think he was dead, shot while
crossing the frontier or while escaping after being captured.
The absolute minimum of people in Russia should know of
his return and an entirely new identity should be arranged
for him in Moscow. He realized that the "Trust" was a GPU
operation, even if many others did not think so—or at least
hoped not. If Dzerzhinsky were to arrange for an invitation
from the "Trust" for a meeting with its leaders, Reilly would
accept, but first he would have to meet with a trusted aide
of Dzerzhinsky on neutral ground in Finland to get written
confirmation from Dzerzhinsky that Reilly's life was not at
risk, that the measures of secrecy and plans for his "death"
were all arranged. On such lines Reilly must have written
to Dzerzhinsky.

In April, a few weeks later, an invitation for Reilly to
meet the "Trust's" leaders in Russia was delivered to Bunakov in Helsinki. Bunakov passed this on to Commander
Ernest Boyce of the SIS in London, and Boyce in turn
delivered the invitation to Reilly, urging him to accept. This
Reilly did, but only in principle. Boyce set the wheels in
motion for a meeting between Reilly and the "Trust," but
Reilly procrastinated; perhaps he was having second thoughts,
or wondered if the assurances he sought from Dzerzhinsky
would be forthcoming. Yet, on further urging from Boyce,
he indicated his readiness to meet a representative of the
"Trust" in Finland, and, depending on the outcome of such
a meeting, he would, if necessary, enter Russia to confer
with the "Trust's" principal leaders. If the assurances he
sought from Dzerzhinsky were not forthcoming, he would
be able to make an excuse for not agreeing to enter Russia.
To help pave the way for the meeting, Boyce had gone to
Paris to confer with General Kutyepov, a former Tsarist
general who led an anti-Soviet movement based in Finland,
and who had great faith in the "Trust." Nevertheless, Reilly,

who had never had much sympathy for White Russian émigrés, crossed over to Paris, at Boyce's request, to meet Kutyepov on September 3rd, 1925. He traveled in the luxury of the Golden Arrow; after all, the SIS was paying! He took Pepita with him; it might be their last few days—and nights—together.

In fact, it was a fortnight after reaching Paris before news came through from Bunakov that a meeting had been arranged with "Trust" representatives.

Reilly left Paris on September 21st, bound for Helsinki, where he was met by Bunakov, who told him that the plans had been changed; Reilly was to meet a senior representative of the "Trust" in Wyborg, near the Russian frontier, on September 24th.

At Wyborg, Reilly met with Alexander Yakushev, whom Reilly knew to be a prominent member of the "Trust." While Boyce believed Yakushev to be a staunch anti-Communist, Reilly had strong suspicions that he was an officer of the GPU.

Yakushev delivered a letter to Reilly signed by several leaders of the anti-Bolshevik underground inviting him to Russia. At the same time, Yakushev must have confirmed Reilly's suspicions and given him the assurances from Dzerzhinsky that Reilly had asked. Otherwise, plans for Reilly's return to Russia the following day would not have been laid; instead Reilly would have made an excuse not to go.

The next night, Reilly, accompanied by Yakushev, secretly crossed the Finnish frontier in the region of Sestroretsk. There they were met by Toivo Vjahi,[2] a senior member of the Border Guards, who must have been brought partly into the secret, if only to the effect that Yakushev would be escorting someone very important across the frontier.

Toivo Vjahi drove the two men in a horse-and-cart to Pargolovo railway station some fifteen miles into Russian territory. At Pargolovo, Reilly and Yakushev boarded a train bound for Leningrad, which they reached the next day.

On the journey Yakushev explained that the "Trust" leaders were expecting Reilly; he would have to meet them near Moscow. The GPU was anxious to maintain the "Trust" in existence; many undercover GPU men—and some women—belonged to it, and it was a perfect institution for keeping a close eye on counter-revolutionary activities both at home and abroad. None of the GPU members of the "Trust," with the exception of himself, could know of the real reason for Reilly's return, and all had been instructed not to harm him.

Once the meeting was over he would be driven to Moscow Station for the journey back to Leningrad and thence Finland. En route for Moscow, his car would be stopped and he would be genuinely arrested by a posse of GPU men but, again, they had been instructed not to harm him. In all probability, Reilly would then be taken to a dacha outside Moscow and remain under house arrest until visited by Dzerzhinsky. A few days later, a fake shooting incident would be staged near the Finnish frontier and a press announcement issued so that the world would think Reilly had been killed.

Almost everything happened as Yakushev forecast it would. According to several unofficial published Russian accounts[3] Reilly duly met the leaders of the "Trust" in a dacha at Malahovka, outside Moscow. Among those present were General Potapov and Alexander Langovoi, commander of the Red Army. The talk was of counter-revolution and the need for funds, which Reilly told the meeting he was sure he could get, once he returned to London. To play the role of a counter-revolutionary, which in effect he had been for several years, was not difficult.

The car driving Reilly back to Moscow was duly stopped by a posse of GPU men, as Yakushev had predicted. Reilly was ordered into another car and driven to a secret hideout—presumably a dacha outside Moscow.

The full details of the manner of the birth of the new Reilly, agent extraordinary of the GPU, are not known. There have been Russian reports that he resurrected the name

Relinsky and also that he worked for the GPU in Leningrad, but these stories do not ring true. The name Relinsky is too similar to Reilly, and it seems unthinkable that Reilly would be posted to Leningrad away from Lubianka Square. Much more probably he was given the highly unremarkable name of Sidorov—another name he is said to have used—and remained in or near Moscow.

For Reilly who had quit Russia, seemingly for good, at the age of nineteen, soon after he had been in trouble with the Tsar's police for carrying Marxist correspondence, the wheel had turned full circle. He was back in the land where he was born, seemingly for good, destined to work for the heirs of Karl Marx.

CHAPTER IV

Better-Laid Schemes

Reilly's debriefing, the manufacture of a new identity for him, and the mapping out of his future role with the GPU, must have been handled in the greatest possible secrecy by Commissar for State Security, Feliks Dzerzhinsky himself, in consultation with Mikhail Trilisser, chief of the INO[1] and Arthur Artuzov, head of the GPU Counter Intelligence.[2] None of the three had had direct experience of Britain and what we now call "The West," and the only form of political regime they had known, apart from Communism, had been that of Tsarist feudalism. Dzerzhinsky, although of Polish aristocratic extraction, had spent the greater part of his life in exile in Siberia to which he had been sent three times. On the first occasion he had been only twenty years old and he bore traces of his exile on his face. My father, who had had dealings with him in 1918, described him as having eyes that "blazed with a steady fire of fanaticism."

The return of Reilly to Moscow marked the most important turning point in the GPU's intelligence strategy abroad. Compared to the sophistication of the world espionage scene of the 1980s, the British intelligence expertise of the 1920s may have been rough-and-ready. Nevertheless, in its techniques and the caliber of its personnel, it was decades ahead of the intelligence resourcefulness of other countries.

The inside knowledge of British intelligence and counter-intelligence techniques, staff, agents, and organization were not the only invaluable assets Reilly brought with him to Moscow. Although these enabled the Soviets to counter, neutralize, or circumvent British Communist-targeted espionage and counter-espionage work, in retrospect, Reilly's actual and intuitive knowledge of the British "establishment" and consequential awareness of the best methods of infiltrating and manipulating some of its components, were of greater value still.

The deviousness and fanaticism of Dzerzhinsky and the inherent Russian capacity for patience, allied to Reilly's flair and wide experience, were the anvil on which the new GPU was forged. The salient outcome was the recruitment of foreign national "moles"—British in particular—and "agents of influence" together with the training of agents for installation abroad as "sleepers." The state security system hitherto largely concentrated against enemies of Communism within Soviet Russia and potential counter-revolutionaries abroad, preened its feathers in preparation for spreading its wings in foreign lands. Dzerzhinsky, with his closest GPU colleagues and with Reilly as an advisory "pilot," set in motion the creation of a brilliant—if fiendish—new concept in intelligence that was eventually to blossom into what Philby has described as an "elite force"—the KGB.

Reilly had been not only on intimate terms with the senior officers of the British intelligence services and the Foreign Office. His charisma, panache, and sheer forcefulness of character had led him to important contacts in political and business circles. He had been equally at home with men and women of the theater and the middle-class "establishment"—or "ruling classes"—generally. He was aware of the growing disillusionment among the young men of Britain destined to become the next generation of "establishment" decision makers.

Whatever may have been Reilly's personal inclinations, he could not have been allowed to live in central Moscow

and roam the city at will. The familiar landmarks to which
nostalgia must have tugged at him such as the Moskva River,
St. Basil's Cathedral with its eight domed chapels each in
honor of a saint on whose day Ivan the Terrible had been
victorious in battle, Pushkin Square, Red Square, and the
gaunt citadel that was the Kremlin, were not for his eyes
to linger on.

Moscow is set in a forested part of the USSR and, as in
most capital cities of the world, it has its fashionable or
quasi-fashionable suburban areas. Here, surrounded by trees
and hidden from enemies' eyes, Reilly would have spent
most of his time in a dacha with domestic help provided by
the GPU. Any boredom he might have felt would be dis-
sipated by regular visits from Dzerzhinsky—and his successors—and other members of the Lubianka Square
hierarchy. In any event, Reilly had always been a man to
revel in the exercise of behind-the-scenes power.

One cannot help but wonder to what extent the Casanova
element in Reilly's character may have missed—or enjoyed—female company on his return to Russia. But the
GPU then—as with the KGB today—was not short of
women operatives who could "entertain." One Soviet media
source I have met in recent years maintains that Reilly
resumed a relationship at this time with Dagmara
Grammatikova,[3] the dancer from the Moscow Arts Theatre
who had been Reilly's mistress in 1918.

The ascension of Stalin to the Soviet leadership after the
death of Lenin in 1924 was followed by the demise of
Dzerzhinsky in July 1926. Lenin and Dzerzhinsky had been
the two men who had contributed to the success of the
Revolution: Lenin, the brain; Dzerzhinsky, the sword. As
was naturally the case for Lenin, Dzerzhinsky, the revered
ancestral father of today's KGB, was also given a state
funeral. The pall bearers were Stalin, Trotsky, Kamenev,
Zinoviev, Bukharin, and Rykov.[4] This must certainly have
been an occasion when Reilly made an appearance—albeit

unobtrusive—in Red Square. One can but speculate on his emotions at the passing of the man who had been first his foe and then his friend and with whom his life had been so interwoven over eight turbulent years.

Dzerzhinsky was succeeded by his deputy, Vyacheslav Rudolfovich Menzhinsky, a lawyer who, like Dzerzhinsky, was of Polish descent. In contrast to the dedication to Bolshevism of Dzerzhinsky, Menzhinsky was essentially an opportunist, and something of a fop who dyed his fingernails red with henna. Yet he gave fulsome praise to his predecessor. Of Dzerzhinsky he said: "He had his special talent which set him apart. He was not guided by any goal except one—the success of the proletarian revolution."

Reilly, too, had his special talents, which had been employed already to considerable effect in the reorientation of GPU strategy. The inevitable jostling for power resulting from the death of Dzerzhinsky created but a temporary hiatus in this reorientation. The GPU's "Reilly Gambit" was soon to be further deployed with far-reaching results.

CHAPTER V

Dealers in Deceit

Before evaluating the extent of Reilly's contribution to GPU strategy and its duration and long-term effects on Soviet espionage and subversion, it is appropriate to summarize the overwhelming evidence that Reilly lived on for at least twenty years after his return to Russia in 1925; and, that during that time he was a major influence on the course taken in Soviet intelligence operations against the free world.

Here then are the facts of the case:

1. Despite his espionage for Britain, Reilly's first allegience, and a deeply emotional one at that, had always been to Russia—the country.

2. Although he appeared to enjoy his periodical excursions into the high life of London, Paris, and New York, Reilly's political persuasions were always very much to the Left.

As a youth he had been briefly involved with a Marxist organization and from 1918 to 1925, he was closely associated with the Social-Revolutionaries who, despite their rivalry with the Bolsheviks, were fundamentally of the same revolutionary ilk.

3. Those who knew Reilly before he returned to Russia have testified to his almost obsessive passion and devious-

ness. He would certainly have concealed the true intentions of his 1925 return.

4.   From the earliest times of his association with British intelligence, MI6 and MI5 officers including Mansfield Cumming ("C"— the head of the Secret Intelligence Service), had suspicions about the direction in which Reilly's true loyalties really lay.

5.   Although Reilly professed to be anti-Bolshevik, his letter to my father extolling Bolshevism tells a different story. (Soviet agent Philby, who went up to Cambridge only four years after Reilly's return to Russia, actively simulated sympathy in the 1930s for two of Communism's dedicated enemies—Hitler's Germany and Franco in Spain. Another brilliant secret agent Sorge—"The Man with Five Faces"— adopted a similar Reillyesque ruse in Tokyo during World War II by posing as an anti-Moscow Nazi.)

6.   Reginald Bridgeman of the Foreign Office maintained that he never thought Reilly to be an anti-Bolshevik as he made out, and that Reilly had always said that in the long run it would be better to join the Bolsheviks than to fight them.

7.   Captain Van Narvig, a Finn, who served on the staff of General Mannerheim and was later partly responsible for the defection to the U.S. of Walter Krivitsky of the GPU, had met Reilly in Finland in the 1920s. Van Narvig confirmed to British author Richard Deacon that Reilly was fully aware that the "Trust" was a GPU operation. According to Van Narvig, Reilly was disgusted with the pro-German attitude of the British Secret Service.

8.   It cannot be emphasized strongly enough that there has never been any official Soviet statement to the effect that Reilly met his death at the hands of the GPU. Every request to the Soviets from Britain—including my own—for information about Reilly has been met with icy

silence. Not even an ambiguous answer has been forthcoming.

9.   The only semi-official (?) answer I have ever received
personally from a Soviet source came from the onetime
London and Washington based Milor Sturua, who told me
that all Soviet records about Reilly had been lost or destroyed. Very convenient!

10.   All published Russian accounts of Reilly's career, although ending in his death by one means or another and at
one place or another or on one date or another, are unofficial
and contradictory. "Death" is the most perfect cover for a
spy or intelligence officer prior to his taking up a new role.
It was not unknown for Soviet agents to have been killed
off *on paper*—usually by "execution" for anti-Soviet activities following "trial" and "conviction" only to be rede-
ployed as a GPU agent under a different name (e.g., Toivo
Vjahi, who emerged forty years after his "execution" as
KGB Colonel Petrov).

11.   Remember, too, that Reilly had faked his own death
by "suicide" as a young man. He himself may well have
suggested his own "death" to Dzerzhinsky.

12.   There is no escaping the fact that in the years following
Reilly's return to Russia in 1925, GPU strategy abroad
underwent a radical change. In addition, a number of British
intelligence officers and agents were compromised or
"blown," and all remaining émigré counter-revolutionary
activity was virtually extinguished.

13.   In any event, it is inconceivable to suppose that were
a master-spy such as Reilly to have entered Russia as a
purely British agent and been taken prisoner, he could have
not only confessed what he knew of British intelligence
organizations, but also actually contributed advice that resulted in major and lasting changes in the GPU's whole
external strategy and then suffer execution—all in the space

of a month, as some unofficial Soviet accounts would have us believe. Had Reilly really been liquidated, there would have been no reason for the Soviets not to have made a formal announcement to that effect.

14.   Unofficial Soviet accounts of Reilly's so-called confessions are riddled with inaccuracies about his life and work. If published with some form of official sanction, this could only have been done for *dezinformatia* reasons.

Revolt Pimenov's close analysis of Soviet writers on Reilly show that both Minaev and Nikulin, the two leading "authorities" with close connections with the Soviet powers-that-be, not only contradicted each other, but in writing on quite different intelligence matters were demonstrably very inaccurate—probably under orders, for *dezinformatia* reasons. (Minaev always followed the party line slavishly and Nikulin spent part of his career in the political departments of the Soviet armed forces.)

Pimenov, in his well-researched *Samizdat*, with access to documents not available to the ordinary Soviet citizen, despite his satire at the expense of the GPU/NKVD, concludes that Reilly was the USSR's greatest spy.

15.   Moura Budberg was most specific when she reported to my father in 1932 that Reilly was still alive. It is clear also that she must have met Reilly in the Soviet Union *after 1925*.[1]

16.   Although he has not revealed classified information to me on the subject, the former MI5 leading "mole-hunting" officer has been quite dogmatic in telling me that Reilly was a double agent who turned over completely to Moscow and, as "The First Man," paved the way for Philby, Burgess, MacLean, and others.

17.   There is the Soviet media source who told me of Reilly's resumed relationship with Dagmar Grammatikova on his return to Russia.

18.   In *Ace of Spies* I mention that Reilly's close colleague
in SIS, the late Brigadier George Hill, who was liaison
officer to the NKVD in Moscow in World War II, had told
me that a member of the British Mission had been informed
by a Soviet official that Reilly was still alive but in prison
and insane. Although I reported this, I did not take it too
seriously, nor do I think Brigadier Hill did.

Only after *Ace of Spies* had been published did I learn
from Hill that he himself had been told by a NKVD major
and also by one of his former 1918 agents[2]—but by the
1940s working for the NKVD—that Reilly was alive and
had been actively working for the GPU and subsequently
for the NKVD. (Hill eventually confessed that he did not
tell me earlier because he did not wish to spoil a good story.)

19.   There is the intriguing unsolicited invitation I received
last year to visit the USSR to meet with a Soviet who could
give me what he believed to be the true inside story of
Reilly—*the Soviet Secret Agent* (an invitation which I re-
gretfully had to refuse for what I hope are obvious reasons).

Reilly can no longer be alive: he was born in 1874. He
must have died sometime after 1945. (In that year, he would
have been only 71.) As in most countries, details of Soviet
secret operations are not normally released until perhaps
fifty years or more after they have taken place—if at all.
The world may never know the complete Reilly story, yet
the possibility that the Soviet authorities might reveal this
to some future generation of readers cannot be discounted.
A number of GPU and NKVD officers, condemned in the
past as "agents of foreign powers" have been "rehabilitated"
a great many years later and revealed to be Soviet heroes.

What we are aware of, apart from the fact that Reilly
lived on, under another name naturally, Siderov perhaps,
for at least twenty years after his return to Russia, is a
dramatic change in GPU overseas strategy after his return.
The "fifth column" cadres established abroad by the GPU

had two prongs: the one concerned with subversive activities and the other with intelligence, political and—overlapping with the Red Army's GRU—military. It goes without saying that in the realm of subversion, infiltration into trade unions, and attempts to create disaffection among armed forces was nothing new; it was not a sphere in which Reilly had any particular expertise to offer. However, when it came to implementing a new policy of seeking out potentially sub-versive "fellow-travelers" either overt or covert, in the po-litical circles of Westminster and in the corridors of power in Whitehall—men who later came to be called "agents of influence"—Reilly's "know-how" was absolutely unique. So was it in the entirely new departure of attempting to infiltrate intelligence services with agents who came to be known as "moles."

This explains why Britain was the first country to be subjected to this new form of Soviet penetration. The ex-perience gained in Britain enabled the GPU and later the NKVD and KGB to repeat the exercise in other countries— in the United States in particular.

There could be no question of Reilly himself being able to return to Britain as a form of "recruiting sergeant"; and in any event, there was the problem of planning similar subversive and intelligence infiltration in other countries. Such new sophisticated operations were well beyond the abilities not only of the average run-of-the-mill GPU officer, but also the senior personnel in GPU headquarters at 2, Lubianka Square in Moscow. Children of the revolutionary melting pot that had turned former Tsarist colonels into Paris cab-drivers and had thrown up railway porters as commis-sars, few had ever been out of the Soviet Union. Most were of humble and uneducated backgrounds, and many were illiterate.

It is axiomatic that Reilly must have counseled the en-rollment of entirely different and superior personnel: ded-icated communists, yes, but men and women of education, high intelligence, linguists and, above all, people who could mix with members of foreign "establishment" classes.

Given that the overall design of the new strategy probably emanated from Reilly's brain, it is most likely that he had some hand in the selection of some of the leading GPU protaganists of that strategy. Certainly in the early stages he must have been consulted, if not by Menzhinsky himself, at least by his two deputies to whom he delegated a great deal: Genrikh Yagoda and Trilisser, who had been promoted following Dzerzhinsky's death while still maintaining his post as chief of the INO (Foreign Department), until Artuzov was moved from running the KRO (counter-espionage department) to head up the INO.

The new-style Soviet agents chosen either directly by Reilly or as a result of his advice and influence were not so much straightforward spies but dealers in deceit who completely changed the meaning of the word *spy*. One such dealer was Leon Feldbin.

CHAPTER VI

Enter Orlov

Everyone knows the old racialist epigram: "How odd of God to choose a Jew." And how odd of the Soviets to persecute the Jews today. One wonders what proportion of Russia's millions realize that the success of the Revolution was in no small measure due to the major Jewish element in the Bolshevik hierarchy; and how many know that Lenin's maternal grandmother was a Jewess? And how many, even among today's KGB personnel, are aware that it was a Jew whom Dzerzhinsky chose to spearhead the new-style Soviet subversion and intelligence advocated by the half-Jewish Reilly in the West in a most spectacular manner.

The young man selected by Dzerzhinsky went by the name of Leon Feldbin. Born in 1895, and come the Revolution a brilliant law student, he joined the Bolshevik party in 1917, changed his name to Lev Lazarvik Nikolsky, and became a junior army officer. In 1920, when still only twenty-five, he had been brought to Dzerzhinsky's personal attention on account of his successes in guerilla warfare and counter-intelligence in Poland.[1]

In the following year, Feldbin Nikolsky was appointed assistant prosecutor of the Supreme Court under Nikolai Vasilyeisch Krylenko,[2] who later became commissar of Justice and the chief prosecutor at the early "purge" trials. Stalin's mouthpiece to be, Vyshinsky, worked in the same court.

Three years later, in 1924, Dzerzhinsky brought the young assistant prosecutor into the expanding GPU to serve in the EKU (The Economic Directorate) where he supervised four departments, including the covert exploitation of foreign business, and also all the EKU's internal secret informers. Feldbin/Nikolsky celebrated his thirtieth birthday with a year's detachment in command of a brigade of 11,000 men of the NKVD Border Guards.[3] But 1926 found him back in Moscow in charge of a new unit within the INO (The GPU's Foreign Department). Hardly had he joined his new unit before he had been short-listed by Dzerzhinsky for the new key post in Western Europe, which the GPU chief must have discussed with Reilly before the former's death in July 1926. Whether Feldbin/Nikolsky knew Reilly personally, we do not know. If he did, he took his views on Britain's ex-master-spy to the grave along with a great many other secrets.

Feldbin/Nikolsky under yet a third name—Leon Niko-layev—was soon on his way to Paris as *resident*[4] in France where he spent two years setting up numerous spy rings and fomenting subversion in the rapidly growing French Communist party without arousing the suspicions of the "Deux-ième Bureau."

Having successfully laid the foundation stones of a so-phisticated new NKVD presence in France from which to-day's KGB's operations were spawned, the head of the French *rezidentura* was transferred to Berlin in 1928 as the NKVD chief for Germany, attached to the Russian Trade Delegation[5] as cover and with yet another name, Alexander Orlov, and it is by this name he is principally known and referred to in intelligence circles.

The year of Orlov's move to Berlin was one which had seen Socialist electoral gains. A Socialist named Herman Muller had become Chancellor. Germany at that time was moving to the Left.

Working through several Russian assistants, Orlov built

up a finely tuned network of separate yet interlocking spy-rings. Each Russian assistant would control a few independent small spy-rings of four or five German communists. At the same time the German Communist party under its leader, Thaelman, was continually canvassed to expand its membership and influence secretly through the establishment of classic *"funfergruppen"*.[6]

In 1931, Orlov returned to Moscow to become head of the EKU. Menzhinsky was still head of the GPU and his two Deputies, Genrik Yagoda, and Artur Artuzov, the architect of "The Trust," continued to be the powers behind the throne. Reilly, with his intimate knowledge of the West, was presumably by now the *eminence grise*, advising on the main strategy the State Security Commission should adopt against the democratic world and on the advisability, or otherwise, of enrolling specific "agents of influence" and "moles" in Britain.

In his new position Orlov traveled frequently and served on a small council of six within the GPU/NKVD to evaluate secret reports from spy-rings abroad for the Soviet Foreign Office and for the Politburo. At least once a week he helped produce similar reports for Stalin. He also wrote a training handbook for the NKVD schools preparing intelligence operators for work abroad and not infrequently lectured at these schools. In addition he was overall director of the intelligence and counter-intelligence section of the NKVD Central Military School.

Young Leon Feldbin, one of the GPU's new "favorite sons," had come a long way.

It is not hard to imagine Reilly, with his resentful disillusionment with America, following his case against the Baldwin Locomotive Company, urging that in the long run the United States, the world's leading capitalist country, would become Communism's main adversary and hence deserved more attention. Orlov succeeded, on the basis of promoting import trade in U.S. automobiles, in obtaining an invitation in late 1932 to spend nearly three months as

the guest of General Motors. Now the ground was laid for
the later appointment of Gusev, one of Orlov's aides, as
rezident for the United States. Gusev was to become largely
responsible for the riddling of the United States government,
armed forces, and scientific research establishments with
Soviet agents. The consequences have been virtually world-
shattering. But America and Orlov were destined to meet
again under very different circumstances.

It was during these years in Moscow, I have been informed by a Russian formerly very closely associated with
the KGB, that Orlov engineered the return to the Soviet
Union of Pyotr Kapitsa, a brilliant Russian scientist with a
growing international reputation. Born in 1895, Kapitsa had
been working with Rutherford at the world-famous Cavendish Laboratory in Cambridge since 1921. Reilly, who
would have studied all official Soviet reports from Britain
and also the British press, must have drawn attention to the
striking news of Rutherford's[7] splitting of the atom in 1932—
even if no one else had. Soviet scientists were much impressed.

There followed several attempts to lure Kapitsa back to
Russia, none of which were successful until in 1935, Orlov
dispatched to Cambridge a bright young NKVD officer who
had barely finished his training to solicit Kapitsa's return
with a combination of promises of a fine laboratory with
all the equipment he needed and a handsome dacha, and of
scarcely veiled threats of the "unpleasantnesses" his family
in Russia might expect if the offer was not accepted. Kapitsa,[8] elected a Fellow of the Royal Society in 1929, told
his Cambridge colleagues that he was only off to Russia for
his annual holidays; but he never returned to Britain.

The young NKVD officer Orlov had sent to Cambridge
was none other than Rudolf Abel (a.k.a. Willy Fischer,
born in Newcastle-on-Tyne according to his birth certificate), who was later to hit the headlines when, as a KGB
colonel, he was arrested by the FBI in New York in 1957,
sentenced to thirty years' prison as a leading Soviet spy,

but exchanged in 1962 for U-2 pilot Gary Powers.

Meanwhile, Communism had been gaining ground in Spain. In the general election of February 1936, the newly formed Popular Front, a conglomeration of left-wing Republicans, Communists, and Anarchists, came to power. In July the Civil War broke out.

One of the first important decisions made by Nikolay Yezhov, who had just taken over the NKVD from Yagoda,[9] was to send Orlov to Spain to advise the Spanish Government on guerrilla warfare and intelligence work.

In Spain, Orlov was engaged in many clandestine operations with numerous Soviet agents working for him, and it was while in Spain that Orlov, on the direct orders of Stalin, arranged for the Spanish Republicans' gold reserves—some 1.5 million pounds of gold—to be shipped "for safety reasons" to Russia. Stalin's reported comment at the time was: "They will never see their gold again, just as they cannot see their own ears."

It was during the Spanish Civil War, too, that Stalin began the merciless purges[10] of his "enemies," potential or imaginary. The firing squads worked overtime, executing thousands who were arrested and tried on trumped up charges of treason. The ranks of the NKVD were by no means exempt from the bloodbath, and, on one of his not infrequent visits to Paris, Orlov learned that senior NKVD officers abroad were being recalled for "consultations" or "holidays," but in reality to be shot or, if lucky, dispatched to gulags.

Orlov was not altogether surprised, therefore, when he received a peremptory cable from Yezhov on July 9th, 1933, ordering him to proceed immediately to Paris and thence by embassy car to Antwerp to board the Russian ship, *Svir*, on July 13th or 14th for important discussions with "a visitor" from Moscow.

NKVD Major General Alexander Orlov, one time Leon Feldbin, had no intention of being lured back to Stalin's slaughterhouse. While cabling Yezhov that he would follow

his instructions and go to Antwerp, Orlov left Barcelona
forty-eight hours later, collected his wife and daughter living
in France just across the border from Spain, and went to
Paris, arriving there on July 13th, the eve of Bastille Day.
After checking in at a hotel, Orlov went directly to the U.S.
embassy only to learn that Ambassador William Bullitt and
virtually all the staff were unavailable, having left the city
in view of the next day's holiday.

Orlov next went to the Canadian embassy, where the
General presented his diplomatic passport and asked for
assistance for himself and his family to enter the United
States "on official business" via Canada. The Canadians
helped him to find passage on a Canadian ship from
Cherbourg and on July 21st, Orlov and his family reached
Quebec and thence by train to Montreal. The General,
being well aware that Stalin might wreak vengeance on
his family still in Russia, took out an "insurance" against
this.

In Montreal, Orlov wrote a thirty-seven-page handwritten
letter[11] to Stalin, with a copy to Yezhov, to the effect that
if anything happened to his mother or to his mother-in-law,
Orlov would publish everything he knew together with a
complete list of all Stalin's chief crimes, including the one
secret Stalin feared would one day come out—and the reason he was murdering so many possible "witnesses"—that
the Russian dictator had, in his younger days, worked for
the Tsar's secret police, the Okhrana. Full details would be
released by his lawyer also, in the event of anything hap-
pening to Orlov himself. Orlov got his own back on Yezhov
by revealing to Stalin important instances where Yezhov[12]
had disobeyed Stalin's orders. Orlov had every reason to
take out such an "insurance." About the time of his defection, the long arm of the NKVD murder squads reached out
to assassinate NKVD and GPU defectors Ignace Reiss in
Switzerland, Krivitsky in Washington, and Agabekov in
Belgium.

* * *

On August 13th, 1938, exactly one month after they had called on the Canadian embassy in Paris, the Orlovs entered the United States. One of the most valuable recruits spawned from "The First Man's" new intelligence hatchery had deserted ship.

CHAPTER VII

•

A Man Called Henri

Semyon Nikolayevich Rostovsky was born in 1904 and joined the Bolshevik party as a teenager. As a young man in the 1920s, he underwent a brief spell in a Berlin prison for subversive activities against the Wiemar Republic and the covert sponsoring of Communist "funfergruppen."[1] According to Soviet sources, he was jailed for assisting "the revolutionary struggle of German workers against those forces of imperialist reaction which later reared as German fascism."

Returning to Russia, Rostovsky was spotted by the INO, the foreign department of the GPU. As a young man of high intelligence, good education, and with linguistic skills, he was directed into Rosta[2] for training in journalism. Rosta was the only news agency in Russia, all others having been suppressed, and was directly controlled by the Council of People's Commissars. Its guidelines, laid down by Lenin himself, included the dictum that "information is the use of facts for the purpose of agitation and for moulding public opinion."

In 1925, the year Reilly returned to Russia, the Soviet government formed a new agency called TASS[3] which absorbed Rosta. The latter then became solely involved in Russian internal news and the manipulation of this while TASS, the parent body, was concerned wholly with overseas news. Rostovsky was switched to TASS and schooled for work abroad.

It was about this time that Rostovsky first made the acquaintance of Ivan Maisky. Another brilliant young man, Maisky was posted to London in May 1925, as counsellor to the first officially recognized Soviet diplomatic mission since Tsarist days.

Maisky returned to Moscow in 1927 when diplomatic relations with the USSR were broken off following a two-hundred-man strong police raid on ARCOS, the Soviet Trade Mission in London. Some evidence of subversive activities was found in the ARCOS headquarters, but it must be admitted that it did not amount to a great deal. Views have been expressed from time to time that ARCOS was tipped off about the raid and that the source of the tip-off was none other than Guy Liddell of MI5, later its deputy director, but I know of no real evidence to this effect. If there was a tip-off, it could have come from anywhere.

The Russian embassy in London was reopened in December 1929, with George Sokotnikov as Soviet ambassador. In the interim, members of the 1927 mission had made their recommendations as regards the course of future Soviet activities in Britain, and these had been considered by the Politburo, as well as by the Russian Foreign Ministry and Reilly and the GPU.

Undoubtedly Maisky's friendship with Rostovsky and respect for his intellect must have contributed towards the placing of Rostovsky on the short list for the post of London correspondent of TASS for consideration by Menzhinsky, or his deputies, in conjunction with Reilly. He fitted the bill ideally as the *agitrop*[5] member of the *apparat*, which the Soviets were starting to build in Eritain. Apart from being a dedicated, hard-working Communist of considerable intelligence, and well-trained for subversive work abroad, Rostovsky had a plentiful supply of personal charm. He was debonair, as meticulous in his dress as in his work, and, yet, could let his hair down and entertain people, playing the guitar, singing Cossack songs, and performing Cossack dances. Here indeed was a man who could mix and be at ease at every social level—an ideal pioneer for the recruit-

ment and opinion-molding to the Communist cause of people of influence in Britain's establishment.

In the early 1930s,[6] not long after the reopening of the
USSR's London embassy in December 1929, Rostovsky
duly arrived in London as official correspondent for TASS,
a perfect cover for his more important work for the GPU.
And through the press connections he established for his
routine news reporting to Moscow, he was soon accepted
among the milieu of young intellectuals with left-wing inclinations.

Rostovsky was an outstanding talent spotter for the GPU,
later the NKVD. He hooked the fish; others played them.[7]
But Rostovsky was always on hand to prevent any of the
catches slipping out of the net when they had qualms about
their new sub-rosa vocations.

In October 1932, Maisky had returned to London, having
relieved Sokotnikov as ambassador. A man much respected
in London's diplomatic world during his eleven-year stay
in London, particularly during World War II, he nevertheless
played his cards close to his chest. It is doubtful if he was
party to NKVD recruitments but, in view of his close relationship with Rostovsky, he was almost certainly privy to
them.

One of the early friendships Rostovsky developed in Britain was with Brian Howard,[8] a communist and a homosexual
who was almost certainly Guy Burgess's greatest friend and,
like him, an old Etonian. Many influences and a number
of people played their part in the recruitment of the hornets'
nest of British homosexual moles, but the "shepherd" who
exerted the most powerful political influence in their recruitment and kept them from straying from the Soviet path
was Rostovsky. It was his job to sustain their loyalty to the
USSR when this might be wavering, as when Stalin's terror
machine was indulging in mass murder. The rather crude
run-of-the-mill GPU/NKVD officer was quite unsuitable for
dealing with Etonian-Oxbridge undergraduates.

In the summer of 1933, under the pseudonym Ernst Henri,

Rostovsky, well-versed both through training and from his experiences in Germany in covertly forming underground subversive Communist *funfergruppen*[9] cells, wrote two articles (see Appendix IV) for the left-wing British periodical *The New Statesman and Nation* expounding and extolling the *funfergruppen* principle.

Subsequently, Brian Howard himself, writing in *The New Statesman and Nation*, having first defended homosexuality, applauded "Ernst Henri's" appeal for "Groups of Five" and recommended that anti-Fascists should take up the idea and band together at once.

The rest is history. Brian Howard's friend Burgess was recruited by the Soviets, Burgess recruited Blunt, and Blunt recruited the American Michael Straight: and these were far from being the only ones to fall for Rostovsky's guile. Reilly's recommendations that the Soviet Union should aim at recruiting agents in high places where they could not only pass on information but influence policy and events was paying off in a big way.

There have been numerous explanations given for the motivations that led the men of Cambridge to betray their country—none altogether convincing. When the "moles" were eventually exposed, there was bewilderment that young men of the "establishment"—men of good family, of public school and university education, sons of the privileged and ruling upper middle classes, should have turned traitors to bite the very hand, so to speak, which had fed them with their privileges. Yet the clue to their treachery surely lies precisely in their privileged backgrounds.

By the 1930s, the British Empire was clearly on the wane. Like all great empires before it, the Empire "on which the sun never sets" had passed its zenith. The power base of the privileged "establishment" class who had provided Britain with its civil servants, colonial governors, admirals, generals, and administrators generally for so long, was eroding. The countless numbers of their sons who had died

leading others into the abattoir of the 1914–18 War; the
Russian Revolution; the liberation of women; the failure of
the politicians to fulfill their promise to build "a land fit for
heroes"; all of this spurred the new generation spawned by
the "establishment" to reconsider the whole politico-social
scene that their fathers had taken for granted. Many of the
young men of the 1930s gradually awoke to the hypocrisy
of their nineteenth-century forebears who had extolled the
triumph of the Industrial Revolution while tolerating the
sending of children to work in the mines and who, while
assiduously attending church on Sundays, almost as assiduously seduced their female domestics. The 1929 Wall Street
crash in the United States seemed to herald the truth of
Marx's prophecy that capitalism was doomed.

With the rise of Adolf Hitler and his ambitions for a
Reich that would last a thousand years, had the millions
who had perished in the muddy trenches of Flanders died
in vain? Despite the bloodshed involved, the French Revolution had led eventually to a democracy—the Napoleonic
era of dictatorship conveniently forgotten. Despite its bloodshed, had not the Russian Revolution freed the people from
the Tsar's tyranny? If Communists were the avowed enemies
of Hitler's Nazi Germany, were they not to be embraced as
friends? The theories of Marx and Lenin had attractions for
a number of disillusioned "privileged" young men. The
Spanish Civil War enhanced Communism's attraction for
many.

In the political and economic turmoil of the 1930s, many
young people felt they had been betrayed by the previous
generation. Yet young undergraduates were the last to be
suspected of treasonable intentions.

Sympathy with Marxist ideas was one thing but betrayal
of one's country was another. Yet, inevitably the goodly
number of sympathizers in the universities—Cambridge, in
particular, where political issues tended to be treated more
seriously than at Oxford—provided a good fishing ground
for the likes of Rostovsky and Cahan. The preponderance

of homosexuals among the Cambridge "moles" can be no coincidence. In the Britain of the 1930s, sexual deviants were quite unable to adopt the openness accorded to homosexuals in today's permissive society; buggery was a criminal offense. As a minority, forced to live out their personal lives in secret, many bore a grudge against a social structure which refused to accept them and were susceptible to Soviet approaches. The subsequent history of twentieth-century espionage has shown that homosexuals make unreliable agents and provide fodder for a blackmailing adversary. Perhaps, also, it is no coincidence that, from the Soviet standpoint, the outstanding man of Cambridge, Harold Adrian (Kim) Philby, was heterosexual.

Of the various Cambridge "moles," the only one whom I knew before the war was Donald Maclean. During the two or three summers immediately prior to the outbreak of war, I used to holiday in Aldeburgh, Suffolk, where Donald's mother, Lady Maclean, his sister, Nancy, and his younger brother, Alan, enjoyed the Maclean summer holiday home. I knew them well at that time. I was headed for Cambridge, whereas Donald had completed his time there and had joined the diplomatic corps. He was the "jewel" in the Maclean family crown, and when he turned up periodically in Aldeburgh, the red carpet came out. Being older than I was, we did not have a great deal in common; but he was friendly enough, very jovial, and exceedingly animated about life in general. Today one would say he seemed on a perpetual "high." Having heard so much about this rising young Foreign Office star, I observed him closely. If I had a criticism of him, it was that he was very pleased with himself—a view subsequently endorsed by Sir John Balfour, British minister in Washington during Maclean's posting there. Balfour described him as "arrogant but efficient."

Later, in 1940, after war had broken out and I was sent to Paris as an assistant to the British naval attaché, I came across Donald at the British embassy. I found him surly, aloof, and supercilious, barely recognizable as the Donald

Maclean I had known in Aldeburgh. Yet, neither in peace nor in war could I ever have imagined him to be a traitor to his country.

When I look back today at my own immediate prewar days at Cambridge, I realize how little I was politically motivated. I recall being anti-Chamberlain on account of his appeasement policy and being anti-Labour Party for their even greater appeasement policies. For a brief period I was the honorary treasurer of the Liberal Party group in my college but, on the political scene in general, I was most aware of those few university's communists whose paths had crossed with mine.

Perhaps knowing rather more about Communism in practice through my father's entanglements with the Bolsheviks in the Moscow of 1918, I was more aware of its dangers than most. In addition, I had been brought up on that superb popular *Daily Mirror* cartoon "Pip, Squeak and Wilfred," in which the anti-hero and bogey-man was an evil-looking, tousle-bearded Bolshevik who was never without a bomb with which he hoped to blow up somebody. For this reason I tended to look at those communists I had come across with a kind of awe, as if they belonged to some strange species from Mars.

The subject I was reading at Cambridge was economics and most, if not all, of my friends who were studying with me were very aware of the adherence to Communism of one or two of the lecturers in the economics school, such as Maurice Dobb and Joan Robinson. Some postwar newspaper suggestions that that grand old man of economics, Professor Arthur Pigou, was a Soviet agent were really laughable. On the other hand, I am surprised that no newspaper or book I have read has ever mentioned the open Communist affiliations of D. L. Burn of Christs's College, whom I used to visit for economics' tutorials.

Among undergraduates, I think I only came across two Communists. One was Pieter Keuneman, a Singhalese with Dutch blood, a third-year undergraduate at Pembroke when

I was a freshman. A brilliant orator and dedicated communist, he became president of the Cambridge Union. I met him again briefly in Colombo during the last war when he was writing for the *Ceylon Daily News*. He went on to become leader of the Marxist-Stalinist Communist party in the Sri Lankan parliament. The only other Communist undergraduate I knew was a young Jewish man at Trinity who was seldom without his badge of loyalty—a red tie. He appeared to be very wealthy and something of a playboy, yet periodically disappeared for a few hours at a time for "secret meetings" with fellow communists, none of whom I ever even set eyes on.

Of course the really dangerous Communists at Cambridge were not those everyone knew about, but the non-card carrying "moles" such as Blunt, Burgess, and Leo Long, who belonged to "The Apostles"—an elitist secret society to which a small number of intellectually active young men joined by invitation only; young men of the "establishment" such as Reilly had advised recruiting. The society is known to have been in existence some hundred and fifty years; two or three new members were admitted each year as others left the university. From its earliest days there was a pronounced homosexual influence among "The Apostles." One of its earliest members was the poet Alfred, Lord Tennyson, whose love for Arthur Hallam is referred to in more than one poem. Other well-known and influential homosexual members have included John Maynard Keynes and Lytton Strachey.

"Higher Sodomy" was the secret phrase adopted by the Society to give expression to its theory that since women were mentally and physically inferior to men, homosexual love was of a higher order.[10] The Society of the Apostles at Cambridge is still extant, although I must make it clear that many of its members have been heterosexual.

Apart from Donald Maclean, the only other Cambridge so-called mole I have met is Michael Straight,[11] but that was not until 1984. Michael, who hails from the rich and

well-known American Straight family, was the man who
confessed to the FBI in 1963 that he had been recruited for
Soviet intelligence by Anthony Blunt. His confession, as
with Blunt's subsequent confessions to MI5, were long kept
secret. In 1983, in his at times moving autobiography *After
Long Silence*, Michael Straight made a public confession.
He tells me that when he went up to Trinity in 1934 there
were about fifty communists at Cambridge in secret cells
with about a dozen in his own cell at Trinity. When he came
down, the university contained some one hundred and fifty
communists in secret cells.

Kim Philby, another Trinity graduate who went up to
Trinity in 1929, was not a member of "The Apostles," but
wreaked more havoc to Western Intelligence than any other
Soviet agent. The identity of his Soviet "control" has yet
to be revealed publicly. Graham Greene has described Philby
as having: "The logical fanaticism of a man who, having
once found a faith is not going to lose it because of injustice
or cruelties inflicted".[12] Of his enlistment in the ranks of
the NKVD/KGM, Philby himself subsequently wrote:[13] "One
does not look twice at an offer of enrollment in an elite
force." Although former MI5 officers believe Reilly paved
the way for Philby and others, it is doubtful there was any
direct connection between Philby and the other moles in the
1930s; Philby was in a special category of his own.

Once Hitler had invaded Russia and the Soviet Union
was at war, Rostovsky doubled his NKVD activities with
the control of an English language daily newspaper *Soviet
News* and a periodical called *Soviet Weekly News* edited
from offices in Grand Buildings, adjacent to London's Trafalgar Square. These publications were strictly propaganda
sheets designed to show how much Russia was doing to
fight off the Nazi hordes and, by implication, how little the
Allies were doing. His senior staff were Russian, the junior
and secretarial staff British. Although there were clear traces
of a Russian accent, Rostovsky spoke fluent English and

had a fine command of the English language. On duty he was meticulous in the extreme, poring studiously over every single word before the next day's issue went to press. One former British member of his staff has stressed to me Rostovsky's closeness to and admiration of Maisky, and of his contempt for Gusev, who succeeded Maisky as ambassador in 1943.

The British who worked for him proclaimed him to be a "life and soul of the party" man who would take his staff to lively meals in Soho, washed down with vodka, Cossack songs, and dancing. This side of his character was in complete contrast to the dour and morose personalities of the other Russians on his staff. However, Rostovsky did not use the air-time given to him by BBC Radio during the war to further Anglo-Russian camaraderies; instead he extolled the NKVD as the world's greatest intelligence service.

Yet, Rostovsky—none working with him knew him to be Ernst Henri[14] as well—was totally reticent about his life away from the office and his office staff. It was known that he had a flat in Hampstead but that was all. He did not appear to have a wife or any girl friends, yet one of the girls on his staff fell in love with him. He used her quite unscrupulously, according to a wartime associate of his, apparently only to get more work out of her, and in the end she committed suicide.

Although I have no evidence that Rostovsky had homosexual tendencies, his association with a number of the homosexual and bisexual British moles suggests this could be a possibility.

In 1979, when Blunt was asked by a British newspaper reporter to state whether or not he had had any connections with Rostovsky/Henri, he replied that he could not make any remarks about his contacts without clearance from the British cabinet offices. The implication, of course, is that he did.

Journalism has come to be a first-class cover for many secret agents operating for many countries. Rostovsky was one of the first and most successful of such agents. It was not for nothing that Reilly had much earlier known the value of using the press for one's own ends—not as a reporter per se—but to "forge" the death of his wife Margaret, and to forge the Zinoviev Letter[15] which, published in the *Daily Mail*, had been a major factor in the fall of the British Government under premier Ramsey Macdonald in 1924.

CHAPTER VIII

Enter the Baroness

Maria Ignatievna Zakrevskaia was born in the Ukraine in 1892. She claimed to be a Countess Zakrevskaia, but she does not appear to have had any right to such a title, although she may have been the great, or great-great granddaughter of Agrafena Zakrevskaia, wife of a governor of Moscow to whom Pushkin wrote poems.

A slim dark-haired beauty, she married Ivan Benckendorff, a well-to-do relation of the Tsarist ambassador in London, who was second secretary at the Russian embassy in Berlin up to the declaration of World War I. They first met in the house of the Russophile British author, Maurice Baring, when she was on a visit to London. Later she was to refer to herself as the Countess Benckendorff, although her husband was but a distant relation of Count Benckendorff.[1]

Back in Russia she bore her husband two children, a boy (Pavel) and a girl (Tanya) during the first two years of the war. The family had a spacious flat in St. Petersburg and a charming country home in Estonia at which Allied diplomats—members of the British embassy in particular—were frequent guests.

Apart from her native Russian, Maria Ignatievna—or Moura as she became known—spoke fluent English, French, Italian, and German, although all of these with a strong Russian accent. Extremely well-read and highly intelligent,

Moura fascinated men not least because, unlike many clever
women, she knew how to listen to men and to become their
confidante.

Then came the February Revolution, and eight months
later the Bolsheviks took over. Murder and loot covered all
Russia and almost overnight the rich became penniless.

Moura's husband was murdered on his Estonian estate on
April 19th, 1919, and in the post-revolution chaos she strug-
gled to bring up two young children in a land divided by
hate. For a time there were jobs to be had, but in August
1918 the Allies made their ham-handed intervention that
brought nothing but disaster both to themselves and to the
White Russians whom they sought to help. Inevitably the
Bolshevik regime became harsher.

It was in 1918 that Moura met my late father, who had
been sent out by Lloyd George as special envoy to the
Bolsheviks. The love affair that developed between them
has been made widely known in my father's writings and
also figures prominently in the Warner Brothers' film *British
Agent* in which Leslie Howard played my father and Kay
Francis played Moura.

It was through Reilly's close friend, George Hill, that my
father first met Moura. He described her as follows:

> It was at this time that I first met Moura. She was then
> twenty-six. A Russian of the Russians, she had a lofty
> disregard for all the pettiness of life and a courage which
> was proof against all cowardice. Her vitality, due perhaps
> to an iron constitution, was immense and invigorated
> everyone with whom she came in contact. Where she
> loved, there was her world, and her philosophy of life
> had made her mistress of all the consequences. She was
> an aristocrat. *She could have been a communist.* She
> could never have been a bourgeoise.

Madame Nina Berberova,[2] who knew Moura well in the
1920s when she was living with Gorki and has written a

biography of her, has this to say of her, despite having considerable reservations about the lies she told:

> She was clever and tough and fully aware of her uncommon abilities. She had a sense of responsibility, and not just in the ways that a woman might be expected to, but across the board. Knowing very well what her own capacities were, she learned to rely on her physical health and energy, and on her considerable charm as a woman. She knew how to be among people, how to live with them, how to choose them and get along with them. There can be no doubt that she was one of the exceptional women of her time.

When the Reilly plot failed and my father was arrested in the Moscow flat he shared with Moura at 19, Khlebry Lane off Arbut Square, and imprisoned, awaiting execution, his chief interrogator was Yacov Peters,[3] Dzerzhinsky's right-hand man and vice chairman of the Cheka. Nevertheless, Moura succeeded in persuading Peters to admit her to my father's cell.[4] There are students of intelligence history who maintain that Moura allowed herself to become Peters's mistress in order to gain access to my father while he was in the Kremlin. This may or may not be true, but there are others who believe that she had been working for the Cheka all along and had duped my father in a Dzerzhinsky agent-provocateur operation. I give no more credence to this last suggestion than I do to the theory of those who hold that the "Lockhart Plot" itself was a set-up planned jointly by Dzerzhinsky and Reilly.

Just as Reilly was eventually to throw in his lot with Dzerzhinsky, so also was Moura Zakrevskaia/Benckendorff (and later Budberg) to become an important tool of the Soviet Security and Intelligence network within a few years of my father's departure from Russia at the end of 1918, when he was exchanged for Litvinov. She was not the first non-Bolshevik political opportunist to change

sides. Stalin himself had worked for the Tsar's secret
police.

In the early part of the 1914–18 War, there had been
ugly rumors that the British would fight to the last drop of
Russian blood, and the British Military Mission in Russia
produced a booklet for distribution to the Russian armies to
counter this sentiment. The Russian interpreter/translator
who assisted was a talented young writer by the name of
Koruli Chukovsky, who was an acquaintance of Moura's.

It was through Chukovsky that in 1918 Moura was introduced to a literary group called Universal Literature,
whose members lived and worked in an atmosphere as totally remote from prerevolution Russia as was equatorial
Africa from the Antarctic. It was here that she first met
Maxim Gorki, the giant of Russian literature who was destined to become the arch-protagonist of Stalinism in the
1930s, and the man whose mistress and secretary she was
to be for some years.

At the first meeting, the then fifty-year-old Gorki seemed
to display a special eloquence in the presence of the beautiful
young woman who belonged to another world. Chukovsky
whispered to her: "He's like a peacock spreading his beautiful feathers."

Moura was quite dazzled, and Gorki was drawn to her
as much by her intelligence as by her physical attractions.
Soon afterwards she became Gorki's secretary, translator,
literary agent and, of course, mistress. She was moving
into the stratosphere of the Bolshevik hierarchy. Gorki,
who had been one of the Bolshevik's main sources of
income before and during the 1905 revolution, was an old
friend of Lenin.[5]

Indeed when, in 1920, Moura foolishly tried to cross the
frontier out of Russia to see her children who had been
evacuated abroad, and was arrested by Frontier Guards, it
was Gorki's intervention that led to her release. And, in
1921, Gorki, suffering from lung trouble, planned to live

abroad in Italy and aimed to take his mistress with him. To assist her to obtain a permit to leave Russia, he recommended to Lenin that Moura be sent abroad as an adviser to the Carnegie Committee, which was providing food for the starving in Russia. From the published Gorki-Lenin correspondence, we learn that Gorki wrote to Lenin on Christmas Day, 1921 as follows:

> It seems to me that we ought to appoint people who can indicate where things ought to be sent and what ought to be bought and, in general, to give impetus to the job and to expedite in every way the despatch of bread and food-stuffs. I should strongly recommend for this role Maria Ignatievna Benckendorff, a woman of great energy and culture. She speaks five languages.

While apparently still very deeply in love with my father, judging by the intensely passionate love letters she wrote to him in the early 1920s[6] and while enjoying the intellectual and sexual pleasures of life with Gorki, Moura began an affair with the then fifty-four-year-old H. G. Wells, who first met her in 1920 with Gorki. On Wells's own admission they first became lovers that year in Gorki's flat.

Already the mistress of Communist Russia's number-one writer, who was to become a great friend of Stalin and who would extol every facet of Stalinism, including forced labor camps, Moura had now also become the mistress of the then crypto-Communist Wells, who was himself, partly through Moura's influence, later blind to Stalin's true nature. In fact, Wells was so taken in by Stalin that of a 1934 meeting with the Soviet dictator, he was naive enough to write:[7]

> A picture had been built up in my mind of a very reserved and self-centred fanatic, a jealous monopoliser of power.... All suspicion of hidden emotional tensions ceased for ever, after I had talked to him for a few

minutes . . . I have never met a man more candid, fair and honest.

All the while, the passionate love letters to my father continued.

As Gorki was now set to leave Russia in the autumn of 1921, the scheming Moura made a marriage of convenience with an Estonian baron by the name of Budberg, thus acquiring a new passport and the ability to leave Russia herself, see her children in Estonia and join Gorki, who was establishing a home in sunny Sorrento. It was not too long before Moura obtained a divorce and Budberg, something of a shady character, disappeared into Brazil—as Reilly had done many years earlier for different reasons.

The love letters to my father continued until, finally, he and Moura met in Vienna in August 1924, for the first time since Moscow days. Of the meeting my father wrote: "She has not changed, the change is in me. I admire her above all other women. But the old feeling has gone." Moura suggested that they should say good-bye forever. . . . This was not to be.

Eventually, in 1929, Gorki returned to Moscow to be close to Stalin, whom he admired so intensely, while the adventuring Baroness made for England to be close both to my father and to H. G. Wells, whose stormy love affair with Rebecca West had drawn to a close in 1924.

Although my father was no longer employed by the Foreign Office, he maintained close connections with it and also, through his new employer, Lord Beaverbrook, the leading politicians in Britain. Wells, the towering figure of English literature of the period, believed that capitalism was heading for a total breakdown and that Soviet Russia would succeed in its aim of world revolution. Through Wells and my father Moura met most of the people who "mattered" and as a result was able to maintain her finger on the pulse of the political and diplomatic worlds. She was exceedingly well-placed to keep Moscow informed of the "temperature" in Britain—and certainly better placed than the first USSR ambassador in London, George Sokotnikov who, along with a staff of three, reopened the London embassy in December 1929.

To Wells and to my father, she seemed persona non grata in Russia and had been unable to return to Moscow with Gorki. Yet she did tell my father that she had met up again with Gorki in 1931[8] and that the latter was convinced that Stalin's terrorism was completely justified. Further, Moura attempted to persuade my father that the "purge" trials in Moscow were by no means faked.

It was in December 1931 that Pepita Reilly's ghosted and over-dramatized story of Sidney Reilly was published and revived intense speculation as to Reilly's fate. It was Moura Budberg who wrote to my father in March 1932 from Estonia, close to the Soviet frontier, to the effect that Reilly *was* still alive.

There can be little doubt that the Baroness was playing both sides against the middle and had adopted a self-assumed role of double agent.

Ever since her arrival in Britain in 1929 and throughout the 1930s, the Baroness vociferously proclaimed to the world at large that it was quite impossible for her to visit Russia. Yet H. G. Wells, on a trip to Moscow in July 1934 to talk to Stalin, learned fortuitously both from the interpreter at his meeting with the Soviet leader and his guide that Moura had been in Moscow only the week before. On observing Wells's utter astonishment, the Russians quickly clammed up and pretended they must have been mistaken. However, Moura was later forced to admit that she had in fact been in Moscow, and in order to explain away her lies produced a rather feeble trumped up excuse about the need to see Gorki.

Maxim Gorki died in June 1936, and only in 1984 was I informed by a senior member of the Russian media that Soviet newsreel material quite clearly showed the Baroness standing beside Stalin at Gorki's funeral. She had been with

Gorki at his deathbed. The same person informed me quite
categorically that Moura had been a Soviet agent.

England had been Moura Budberg's home from 1929 until
she returned to Italy shortly before her death on October
31st, 1974. In London, she had homes in Ennismore Gardens and in Cromwell Road.

In 1967, when I was writing *Ace of Spies*, I asked for
Moura's help over one or two details about Sidney Reilly,
whom she had known since 1918. I showed her a draft
typescript of the part of the book that covered the events of
1918. The Baroness did her level best to try to persuade me
to delete the references I had made to Bolshevik atrocities
during the Revolution, claiming that these were lies. (In
fact I obtained the horrific details from the Public Records
Office, from reports of the Red Cross, of an English priest,
and of neutral observers.)

I was surprised—perhaps I should not have been—at
Moura's totally noncommittal attitude about Reilly himself.
At that time I was unaware that she had known in 1932 that
Reilly was still alive. How much more did she know?

CHAPTER IX

The George Hill Factor

Readers of *Reilly: Ace of Spies* will recall that one of Reilly's closest associates in Moscow in 1918 and a subsequent colleague and collaborator of his in Britain's SIS was Captain George Hill. Hill (Code name "I.K.8") had been brought up in Russia, spoke several languages like a native, and before he teamed up with Reilly in 1918, had been in Russia collecting intelligence on German troop movements for the DMI (Director of Military Intelligence) at London's War Office.

A man of considerable resource and bravery,[1] George Hill had been dropped many times behind enemy lines and had successfully organized bands of guerrillas consisting mainly of ex-Tsarist officers to operate behind the German lines. Come the Russian Revolution, he had established friendly relations with Trotsky, the Bolshevik minister of War, becoming his unofficial "adviser" on Air matters, and helping him to form his own intelligence service. Like Reilly, Hill had a predisposition for the opposite sex and, apart from collecting a succession of mistresses, was married four times in the course of his life.

Soon after the outbreak of World War II, Hill joined SOE[2] and was the chief instructor at the first school set up to train agents in sabotage. An early visitor to the school was the American Colonel Bill Donovan, who was to become head of OSS (Office of Strategic Services, forerunner of the CIA),

the U.S. counterpart of SOE, and who was to establish
training schools based on what he had learnt from Hill.

In 1940, in the belief that the USSR would eventually
enter the war on one side or the other, Hill also established
an embryo Russian section of the SOE. When Hitler gave
the signal for "Barbarossa"[3] in June 1941, within a few days
SOE put up a proposal, via the Foreign Office, that it should
send a small liaison mission to Moscow, and that a similar
Russian mission should come to London.

Only two weeks later, Molotov agreed to the suggestion
and asked that a SOE officer should visit Moscow to
discuss the idea. In view of the part Hill had played with
Reilly in the counter-revolutionary plot of 1918, SOE did
not consider it politic to propose sending Hill. Another
officer, who had no earlier connections with Russia, was
sent to open discussions. In the event, it was agreed that
a small mission of three SOE officers should be sent to
Moscow while a three-man NKVD mission should be
established in London. To the astonishment of everyone,
including Hill himself, from the short list of names put
forward by the British, the NKVD expressed a firm pref-
erence for Hill as chief of the SOE mission. The Soviet
choice seemed extraordinary seeing that it was Hill who
had been Reilly's most trusted and trusty colleague in
1918, and who, after escaping, had subsequently been on
spying missions with Reilly to Russia in 1919 to foster
General Denikin's White Russia movement, and again in
1920. Who made the decision to accept Hill and why?
According to Hill, Molotov told the British ambassador,
Sir Stafford Cripps, with a rare smile: "We know all about
Captain Hill.[4] There are dossiers so high of his doings
but the NKVD are prepared to accept this officer, as they
know he is an expert."

In 1941, were Reilly still alive he would have been sixty-
seven. That Beria, the NKVD chairman, would have consulted Reilly about the wisdom of accepting Hill seems
obvious. In all probability, Stalin was personally consulted

also. Officially, it had been Molotov who had given the approval; but Molotov was no more than Stalin's mouthpiece—a factor that certainly accounted for his long reign as Soviet foreign minister.

Hill spent four years in Russia as liaison officer with the NKVD,[5] for most of the time in Moscow; but when the German army was menacing Moscow he was evacuated temporarily, along with many Soviet Government officials, to Kuybyshev on the Volga. His two assistants on the three-man team were Major Truskovski, a British naturalized Pole (wished on Hill despite his fierce opposition to having anyone with Polish connections, a factor that might impede the establishment of good relations with the Russians), and a Lieutenant George Graham of the Army Intelligence Corps.

The SOE mission's principal contact in the NKVD was a Colonel Ossipov—Hill doubted whether it was his real name. Throughout the whole period of his mission in Russia, it was rare that he was not under surveillance by NKVD men—the "Y M C A boys," Hill called them—or by an NKVD or "Y W C A" lady siren.

From the overall standpoint of the war effort, the SOE and NKVD liaison missions made minimal contributions. George Hill, or Georgei Feodorovich as the Russians called him, was ever puzzled why on earth he had been readmitted into Russia after being persona non grata for twenty years. Objectively he realized that he had considerable expertise to offer the Russians in the field of guerrilla warfare—an area in which the Soviets were weak on the ground following the decimation of their military and NKVD hierarchy during Stalin's monstrous repressions of the 1930s. Yet in view of his former close association with Reilly, he was much puzzled at being in his present post.

Inevitably Hill's thoughts frequently turned to his earlier Russian adventures and to the riddle of Reilly's disappearance in 1925. He realized the uselessness of trying to get any real answer to the sixty-four-thousand-dollar question from one of his NKVD opposite numbers without having

first succeeded in cultivating a genuine and close friendly
relationship with Ossipov and, if possible, some of his colleagues. For most of the time Ossipov, who spoke both
English and German excellently, and Wissarionovich, one
of his principal aides, while normally always friendly, preserved a distance in their relationship with the British mission which made the creation of any real friendships very
difficult.

At the British embassy—the Haritosenko Palace, once
the home of a Tsarist sugar baron—Ambassador Sir Stafford
Cripps and his staff had heard no news of Reilly and thought
it indiscreet to make enquiries of the Narkomindel.[6] Nevertheless, towards the end of the war and as already referred
to in *Reilly: Ace of Spies*, a member of the British Mission
did tell Hill that he had heard from a NKVD contact that
Reilly was still alive, in prison but insane.

Hill doubted very much whether this was a reliable report.
However, it was the spur which made him finally put some
direct questions about Reilly to Ossipov. Ossipov professed
total ignorance of Reilly but later said it was not a subject
he could discuss. Hill became more and more convinced
that Reilly still lived, and that it had indeed been Reilly
who had been instrumental in influencing Beria into accepting Hill as head of the liaison mission.

According to Hill's own unpublished written account[7]
of his liaison years with the NKVD and further information
he gave me shortly before his death, it was not long after
he had questioned Ossipov about Reilly that Hill ran into,
seemingly accidentally, one Sergei Nekrassov, a former
Tsarist cavalry officer who had been Hill's star agent in
1918. Nekrassov told Hill that he had "reluctantly" come
to terms with Communism. Over a bottle of French
brandy—rare in wartime Moscow—which Nekrassov produced, Hill's former agent told him that Reilly was indeed
still alive and had been doing extremely valuable work
for the GPU and then the NKVD ever since he had arrived
in Moscow in 1925. However, Hill was suspicious that

his meeting with Nekrassov had not been as accidental as it seemed, and the French brandy was also an oddity. Nekrassov, Hill felt, was probably an agent-provocateur of some kind. If so, what was the object of telling Hill that Reilly was alive and working for the NKVD? In Hill's mind, the solution appeared to be that it was intended that he *should* consider Nekrassov to be an agent-provocateur and therefore discredit his story that Reilly was still alive; ergo, Hill would believe Reilly to be dead. A question of double bluff and just one more smokescreen to hide the fact that Reilly had lived on after 1925 working for the Soviets.

But it was Ossipov himself who, in May 1945, when the war in Europe was over and just before Hill was returning to England, his tongue perhaps loosened by vodka at a farewell party for Hill, vouchsafed that Reilly really had been working for the NKVD, and that he knew him to have been very much alive up to early 1944.

Beyond that Ossipov could not or would not provide further information. That Reilly should reveal himself to Hill the latter realized would have been out of the question. That was something Beria would never have permitted.

When Hill bid farewell to Ossipov he asked for an address to which he could write him; Ossipov refused to give him one:

"Quite unnecessary," he said. "If our respective organizations wish us to keep contact or work together, communications will be arranged through official channels."

Hill did not tell me the full story of his time in Moscow in World War II—in particular of his conversation with Ossipov and Nekrassov—until after *Ace of Spies* had been published. To me, he appeared to be alternatively questioning, and then convinced, of the premise that Reilly had been still alive during the Second World War. At the time of his death, I had not discovered Reilly's letter to my father extolling the virtues of Communism, nor the evidence of Moura

Budberg that Reilly had been alive in the 1930s. Nor had
the full extent of Soviet penetration into the British intelligence services, implying a directing hand in Moscow, come
to light.

CHAPTER X

Marching As to War

Ribbentrop to Schulenburg   *Berlin: June 21, 1941*

1.) Upon receipt of this telegram all of the cipher material still there is to be destroyed. The radio set is to be put out of commission.

2.) Please inform Herr Molotov at once that you have an urgent communication to make to him and would therefore like to call on him immediately. Then please make the following declaration to him. ... Please do not enter into any discussion of this communication. It is incumbent upon the Government of Soviet Russia to safeguard the security of the Embassy personnel.[1]

At daybreak on June 22nd, Count Schulenburg[2] called on Molotov in the Kremlin who listened to the German ambassador without interruption and said: "It is war."

The evidence that Reilly threw in his lot with the Soviets in 1925 would appear incontrovertible when taken in conjunction with Hill's evidence that he was alive in World War II and with other factual and circumstantial evidence to which reference has been made already. To attempt to reconstruct Reilly's life during the years of the Second World War poses a difficult yet tantalizing task.

Despite warnings from Britain and that brilliant Tokyo

spy, Richard Sorge, and GRU reports of Wehrmacht con-
centrations along the Soviet frontier, Stalin and the Russian
high command were skeptical that Hitler intended to invade
and break the Ribbentrop-Molotov pact. For Reilly it must
have been a traumatic time. As he had been heavily involved
with British intelligence and subversive efforts against Russia and subsequently in intelligence work for Russia against
Britain, one can only guess at what went through Reilly's
mind when he realized that Britain and Russia were now
allies.

Reilly must have wondered whether the callow high command of the Soviet army could match up to Hitler's experienced generals and whether the rank and file of the officer
corps were capable of leading their men in war. The huge
punitive *apparat* established by Stalin in the 1930s resulted
not only in the bloody destruction of millions in the name
of *Repressiya*³ but devastated the army. Up to forty thousand
Russian Red Army officers were liquidated including most
of those of the rank of colonel and some ninety percent of
the generals. It is a wonder that during the period when,
owing to the inefficiency of penal buildings, hotels, mu-
seums, stables, and monasteries had been turned into prisons
and execution chambers, Reilly did not consider redefecting
back to Britain. It is also a wonder that he survived Stalin's
Great Purge of the 1930s at all when some twenty million
Soviets were killed or exiled and when some eight million
were in prison camps at any one time. Catlike, Reilly seems
to have had nine lives.

A few blocks from the Kremlin, where, with the outbreak
of war, Stalin and Marshal Timoshenko, the Soviet commissar for Defence held numerous conferences, lay the
NKVD Headquarters at 2, Dzerzhinsky Square. Here,
alongside the dreaded Lubianka⁴ prison whose walls must
have echoed to more screams of the tortured and of those
awaiting execution than any other prison in history, the war
could not have been many days old before Beria⁵ together
with Vladimir Dekanozov, head of the INO since 1939 would

have redrawn the parameters of Reilly's NKVD brief.

Three German armies were attacking on a long front all the way from the Baltic to the south: von Leeb in the north, von Bock in the center, and von Runstedt in the south. They were driving deep into Russia—particularly in the center. This was where Reilly's idol, Napoleon, and Germany in the First World War, had mounted their greatest pressure— in the Vilna—Smolensk—Moscow direction. The NKVD had to adapt quickly to war. Maslennikov's and Yatsenko's[6] Border Guards administered by the NKVD were ranged alongside the Red Army. Chernyshov,[7] of counter-intelligence, was busy rounding up German nationals and suspected Nazi spies, while additional NKVD officers were being assigned to all Soviet military units to keep watch on the troops' loyalty and to deal with any signs of possible defections or political deviations. Agents abroad and in German-occupied territories were instructed to concentrate on military intelligence and to cooperate with the GRU. But what of the relationship with Russia's new ally—Britain? In what sort of role would Reilly now be deployed?

With all the momentous demands of war, one wonders how much of his time Beria gave to thinking about the usefulness of Reilly and of the various "moles" emplaced in Britain, in the new situation in which Britain had become an ally—at least for the duration of the war.

I like to think of Reilly, before the month of June 1941 was out, being escorted by one of Beria's aides up the private stairs to Beria's office guarded by two white-gloved NKVD officers with tommy-guns; of Reilly entering the commissar's office with its bronze statue of Lenin in one corner, its walls bare except for a huge portrait of Stalin; of Reilly having a one-to-one discussion with Beria on his new brief across the NKVD's chief's large desk beside which stood a small table with a battery of telephones.[8]

In his time, Reilly must have climbed those private stairs more than once for meetings with successive heads of the GPU and NKVD.

The exact nature of Reilly's wartime brief is a matter of conjecture but the broad outline can be readily deduced. With Stalin wishing to enlist maximum help from Britain in the form of a Second Front in Europe as soon as possible together with more supplies for Soviet armed forces, Reilly's advice would have been sought over the preparation of new directives for Soviet agents in Britain, including those with deep cover in positions of influence, such as Burgess, Philby, and Blunt.

Russia was aware of the resistance and sabotage movements in German-occupied Europe which were supported and orchestrated by London. Could Reilly have been instrumental also in obtaining inside information on these underground movements which would help the Soviets organize similar operations behind the German lines? Clearly, of even greater importance was the need to obtain access to all British intelligence on German military intentions and strengths either through normal liaison pipelines—inevitably limited—or clandestinely through such channels as Philby and Blunt could provide. Equally clearly, Rostovsky and his "agents of influence," such as the Cambridge "moles," should help spearhead Soviet propaganda in Britain. In all these areas Reilly's devious mind must have been put to work.

Today, we know only too well how Soviet moles fed intelligence to Moscow, and we can recall how successful Russian propaganda, orchestrated by Rostovsky, from his headquarters by Trafalgar Square, lined up British public opinion behind the USSR. The excesses of Stalin's murder squads of the 1930s were forgotten; "Uncle Joe" was the greatest hero in a land of heroes; a large section of the British public was led to become privately ashamed that the Second Front took so long in materializing.

As for guerrilla warfare, Reilly was not a specialist in this field. He realized how much the expertise of an Orlov was needed, but Soviet intelligence channels had learnt that George Hill was now working for SOE, and there can be no doubt that Reilly persuaded Beria to call for Hill to head an SOE mission to the NKVD. Hill had been a pioneer in sabotage behind the enemy lines in World War I.

Not long after the German invasion of Russia, a groundswell arose in the corridors of Whitehall to appoint my father as ambassador in Moscow.[9] Could such an idea have originated from Reilly? I do not know, but it would have been typical of Reilly to try to recreate the Reilly–Bruce Lockhart–Hill triumvirate of Moscow of 1918. In the event, M. Maisky, the Soviet ambassador in London advised Foreign Secretary Anthony Eden that such an appointment would not be acceptable. Although he, Maisky, had the greatest respect and regard for Bruce Lockhart, Stalin and Molotov were opposed to the idea. How could one explain to the Russian people the appointment as ambassador of someone whom the Soviet press and radio[10] had vilified for years as an arch-enemy, head of the counter-revolutionary "Lockhart Plot"of 1928 and condemned to death in absentia by a Soviet court?

Just as Reilly had made his presence felt in no uncertain manner in World War I, so did he do so in the Second World War—but even more secretly. The total extent of his influence in both wars will never be known.

CHAPTER XI

The Orlov Legacy

In April 1953, General Alexander Orlov "surfaced," choosing to do so in a highly dramatic manner through a series of articles published in four consecutive issues of *Life* magazine: "The Ghastly Secrets of Stalin's Power."

Stalin was not long dead, Orlov was running short of money, and he gauged that both his mother and his mother-in-law—the Orlovs's closest relatives—must be dead and beyond any "vengeance" the Soviets might wish to wreak by way of reprisal for the General's denouncements of Stalinism. The articles gave a detailed insight into Stalin's ruthless barbarism, the fake trials, the murders of the Russian leader's closest associates, and of countless others whom he suspected might possibly know of his evil doings. Among other things, Orlov made it clear that Vyshinsky, then permanent USSR representative at the United Nations and the principal prosecutor at the so-called purge trials, was Stalin's compliant mouthpiece, knowing full well that those he was arraigning were totally innocent.

The general public in the United States soaked up Orlov's every word. One American citizen was so stunned—not by the articles themselves but by the fact that Orlov had surfaced at all—he nearly had an apoplectic fit. The man was FBI chief, J. Edgar Hoover.

How was it possible that a top NKVD general could have arrived in the U. S. without his knowledge? And how could he have lived in America for nearly fifteen whole years while the FBI remained in blissful ignorance? How had Orlov managed to support himself and his family all this time?

Undoubtedly a number of officials in more than one U. S. government department felt the sting of Hoover's wrath, but it was Orlov himself who was to suffer the most. The general underwent lengthy interrogation by the FBI, who learned that since their arrival in the United States, in 1937, the Orlovs had lived in Philadelphia, Los Angeles, Boston, and Cleveland, changing names periodically. Most of the time they were in Cleveland where Orlov was known as Alexander Berg.[1]

Hoover's men soon found out that the Orlovs had entered the United States with $22,800; that he claimed never to have registered for employment nor to have undertaken any paid work lest his name and whereabouts became known to U. S. official circles, which he knew to be pierced by Soviet agents and sympathizers. Despite his "blackmail" letter to Stalin, he realized that the long arm of the NKVD—later KGB—might reach out to the U. S. and bring about his assassination.

Hoover would, at first, have none of this. It was not possible, he asserted, for a family to live for fully fifteen years in the United States with only $22,800. The FBI investigators were told to dig further, to query every dollar the Orlovs had spent since 1937, and to check their annual expenditure on food consumption against prices ruling in every year from 1937 to 1953.

The FBI went to work on this mammoth-sized task. It was found that the Orlovs had been living, as one former U. S. intelligence officer put it to me, "on cats' meat," cheap fish, cheap tinned food, cut-rate scraps, etc. At the end of its investigation, the FBI concluded that it was just possible for Orlov and his wife[2] to have eked out an existence over the well-nigh fifteen years on the money with which they had entered the U. S. In fact, at the time General Orlov "surfaced," he was just about down to his last hundred dollars, and for the previous month he and his wife had been living on nothing but breakfast cereals.

Although certainly nothing like a KGB interrogation accompanied by torture, Orlov was not amused by the tough grilling he received from the FBI. And the FBI having at last finished with him, he was scarcely less upset when it was the turn of the CIA to put him through the hoop.

There is no question but that had the FBI and the CIA handled Orlov differently, he could have revealed a great deal more about Soviet secret activities in the United States. Infinitely more damaging, however, was the fact that the FBI had been kept in ignorance of Orlov's arrival in America in the first place.

In September 1955, and again in February 1957, Orlov appeared before the U. S. Senate Internal Security Subcommittee of the Judiciary. The proceedings were not made public until August 1973, after Orlov's death.

Chairman of the Senate subcommittee was Senator James O. Eastland of Mississippi who, in his introduction to the 1973 published report entitled "The Legacy of Alexander Orlov," referred to him as "the highest-ranking officer of the Soviet State Security (now the KGB) ever to come over to the side of the Free World."

"No man," the Senator went on, "ever testified from a greater fund of knowledge," and Orlov certainly expounded in detail on Stalin and NKVD terrorism as he knew it up to the late 1930s. Further, he warned America that those in power in Moscow since Stalin's demise had not changed Soviet policy either at home or abroad:

> In the aspect of foreign policy, they continue the same policy of Stalin of striving to subjugate other countries and other peoples.

In conclusion, Senator Eastland wrote: "We owe it to Alexander Orlov not to forget him. We owe it to ourselves not to forget his warning."

However, the "Legacy" left by Orlov was not so much

his testimony on the crimes of Stalin and the NKVD, and his warnings of the dangers to the world of Communism. The real legacy lay in the fact that his very existence in the U.S. had been forgotten for nearly fifteen years, between 1938 and 1953. The general testified to the Senate subcommittee as to the NKVD presence in the United States in 1938:

> There was here a chief director resident of the NKVD, by the name of Gusev, a man who had been in former years my assistant. Then Gusev had six assistants. Each assistant had three American assistants, from the Communist party usually, who were the contact men with the spies in the United States.
>
> Each of the Russian assistants took care of at least three rings. So you multiply three rings by six assistants and that makes eighteen rings, eighteen spy rings.

and:

> The most technical engineers were placed high up in all the most secret departments of American defence.

Orlov continued in his 1957 testimony to point out that during the war, when America and Russia were allies, "Russia had the greatest ease of planting spies here," and he drew attention to the spying potential of the embassies[3] and consulates of Soviet satellite countries: "Consulates and embassies have always been covers for Soviet espionage." He also underlined the fact that the eighteen spy rings operating in the U. S. in 1938 to which he had earlier referred excluded those run by the Intelligence arm of the Soviet Army.

> I must say that Soviet intelligence services are the most skillful in the world"—helped "by the complacency of the Western Governments."[4]

Clearly between 1938 and 1953 when he surfaced, the NKVD spy rings had greatly increased from eighteen, to say nothing of those run by the GRU[5] and Soviet satellite countries.

At the time Orlov testified to the Senate Internal Security Subcommittee in 1957, only two major Soviet spy rings had been exposed in the U. S.—those of Whittaker Chambers and Elizabeth Bentley. Orlov stressed that with the lapse of years, which involved new spy rings and changes of Soviet personnel, he was no longer in a position to name anyone engaged in espionage in America, nor to name any Communists in the U. S. government. Whether this statement was true or not we shall never know. He did bear witness to the "tremendous help" the NKVD had received from the American Communist party.

Had Orlov been questioned and his cooperation sought in 1938 when he arrived in New York and was ripe to tell all, who knows what the result might have been. One can be certain that Gusev, one of Orlov's own former aides and chief of the NKVD *rezidentura* in the U. S. at the time, would have been mopped up along with many other Soviet agents. Orlov could have alerted the West to "enemies within" such as Philby, Blunt, Burgess, and Maclean and possibly the resulting greater degree of vigilance and general alertness to Soviet penetration might have led to the activities of atomic spies such as Fuchs, Nunn May, Pontecorvo, and others being nipped in the bud.

If American intelligence officers feel that the British had made one of their greatest blunders in the handling of the Blunt case, they freely admit that their own dealing with Orlov was abysmal. We live with the consequences today.

General Orlov had been paid $44,500 by *Life* magazine for his 1953 articles and these subsequently formed the basis of a successful book. In 1956, he wrote for *Life* again and managed to earn a reasonable living with his pen; his book

The Handbook of Intelligence and Guerilla Warfare, which
he had begun in the 1930s while a senior NKVD chief in
Moscow, was published in 1963.

Orlov and his wife made their home in Cleveland, un-
molested by the KGB, Khrushchev himself having by then
exposed Stalin's crimes to the Russian people. In Cleveland
he made many friends, and, as a result of a private bill
introduced by Senator George H. Bender of Ohio, NKVD
General Orlov became a United States citizen.

On March 25th, 1973, Orlov told the superintendent of
his apartment block at 11406 Clifton Boulevard in Cleveland
that he was not feeling well. The superintendent called an
ambulance and the general was taken to St John's Hospital
on Detroit Avenue, where he was attended to by the house
physician, Dr. Konanabulli, who got in touch with Orlov's
personal physician, Dr. Henry Zimmerman.

A few days later, on April 1st, Dr. Zimmerman arranged
for his patient to be moved to St Vincent's Hospital; but at
9.30 A.M. on Saturday, April 7th, 1973, NKVD Major General Alexander, born Leon Feldbin, a.k.a. Lev Nikolsky and
Leon Nikolayev, succumbed to a heart attack. He was cre-
mated and his ashes buried at Auburn Cemetery, Mount
Auburn, Cambridge, Massachusetts, alongside his beloved
wife, Maria, who had died in 1971 after their golden wedding anniversary, and his daughter Vera, who had died soon
after the Orlovs's arrival in the U. S.

Orlov died intestate and his estate, valued at $47,462,[6]
was handled by attorney George Lowy of Standard Building,
Cleveland, Ohio.

Being intestate, the matter of probate had to be dealt with
by a Judge. In this case it was Judge Ralph S. Locher,
whose attention was drawn to a mass of files found in
Orlov's apartment. The general had been a "string-saver,"
and every scrap of correspondence, bills, personal papers,
etc., on all transactions had been kept; no less than twenty-
three yards of files were found! Judge Locher took one look
at the files and decided that they undoubtedly contained

intelligence-sensitive matters. Under a transmittal order the Judge dated October 23rd, 1974, General Orlov's files were placed in the U. S. National Archives, sealed up for twenty-five years (until 1999).

CHAPTER XII

Return of the Man Called Henri

While Orlov had been lying low in Cleveland and elsewhere in the United States, on the other side of the Atlantic, Rostovsky—could Orlov have exposed him?—had been shepherding the British "moles." And before Orlov surfaced, Rostovsky was back in Moscow.

Publication of the daily *Soviet News* and of *Soviet Weekly* continued for some time after the war under Rostovsky's direction, but eventually the daily paper was closed down while *Soviet Weekly* continued on its own. Publication headquarters were moved from Grand Buildings to Rosary Gardens in the Kensington area of London, where it still operates today.

Rostovsky was exceedingly fortunate to have escaped "elimination" by Stalin's mass terror machine, which had been the lot of virtually every Soviet agent of any importance who had worked in the West for any length of time—to complement, so to speak, the ruthless purges of thousands of GPU/NKVD personnel in Russia itself. Semyon Nicolayevich was left in comparative peace in London; he was far too valuable as a political shepherd to the British "moles"—Maclean in particular.

When, in 1951, Burgess and Maclean were warned by Philby that the net was closing in on them, they fled post-haste to Russia, and the good "shepherd" Rostovsky, on a directive from Stalin, was ordered by Abakumov,[1] then head of the MGB,[2] to return to Russia at once.

Reluctantly Rostovsky complied. In Britain, MI5 and MI6 were thoroughly alarmed following the Burgess and Maclean debacle and, with Philby, Blunt, and other Soviet agents still undetected, there were MGB fears that the British might rumble Rostovsky and that agents might be arrested. For good measure, on his return to Russia, Rostovsky was immediately exiled to a labor camp—small thanks for a hardworking Soviet agent but, to the extent that he was not executed like thousands of others, he was lucky.

After Stalin's death, Kruglov, who had succeeded Beria[3] as head of the MVD, arranged for Rostovsky's "rehabilitation." On his return to Moscow, Rostovsky resumed the role of journalist, wrote for the press and in the following years published various books, translated into several languages, which were full of communist propaganda.[4] In addition he soon resumed relations with Donald Maclean, who now went under the name Mark Petrovich Frazer in Russia.

A traitor dissident in the West, Maclean, although given the KGB rank of colonel and awarded the Order of the Red Banner, was to some extent disillusioned with life in the USSR, and nearly became a dissident behind the Iron Curtain. It was part of Rostovsky's work to continue to "shepherd" Maclean from straying too far from the party line, as indeed it was his task to keep an eye on other leading Soviet figures, such as Solzhenitsyn, who had "dissenting" tendencies.

As I have already pointed out, many countries recognize journalism to be an excellent cover for intelligence work—none more so than the USSR. In the case of the Soviets, where the authorities are ultra-cautious as to whom they allow out of the country in any event, the majority of those working abroad for the Soviet media are at least part-time agents. The Russian journalist Vladimirov who defected to the West claims that most of the Soviet journalists belonging to covert *apparats* work under the aegis of one or the other of the two main news agencies, TASS or Novosti (APN).

* * *

Espionage, disinformation, subversion, and propaganda operations overlap, but combine in the ceaseless pursuit of the Soviet Union's primary goal—Communist world domination. And, despite the USSR's history of military interventions, much progress towards this goal has been achieved without a shot being fired. The Russian press[5] plays a major role in all the areas of espionage, disinformation, subversion, and propaganda. Foreign correspondents and publications in foreign languages make their presence felt in well over one hundred countries. One of the declared aims of Novosti, for example, is:

> To uncover the activities of enemies of peace and of Socialist progress . . . to unmask ideological deviants whether or not they are the normal bourgeois enemies or new traducing types such as Solzhenitsyn's friends, Zionist racists or Peking's new fabricators.[6]

Melor Sturua,[7] to whom I have already referred and the London correspondent of *Izvestia* at the time I was writing *Ace of Spies*, was one of the most intelligent men I have met. Impeccably dressed, like a banker, and with perfect manners, he always managed to out-debate me in the course of several amicably conducted discussions on my criticisms of the Soviet system. I was not surprised when a member of MI5 and U. S. intelligence officers told me of his KGB connection.

Rostovsky celebrated his eightieth birthday in 1984. A leading member of the Soviet Writers' Union, he is still a fairly regular contributor to the periodical *Literaturnaya Gazeta* and inquiries I have made recently have revealed that he remains an active agent of the KGB, still a force to be reckoned with.

The man whom Sidney Reilly was originally responsible for sending to England is, even in his old age, avoided by those in Moscow who know of his continuing association

with the KGB. On two separate occasions in recent years
I have asked members of the Russian media some quite
innocent questions about Rostovsky with surprising—or
perhaps not so surprising—results. In the first instance,
after being told something about Rostovsky's work for the
Literaturnaya Gazeta, a day or two later—clearly on instructions from above—total ignorance about him was professed. On the second occasion, I was told firmly: "I cannot
discuss him." When I asked why not, I received the same
answer and the conversation was immediately changed.

Rostovsky's memoirs, if they were to relate all the detailed experiences of his long career, would make fascinating
reading indeed. Perhaps something will be published after
his death, but even then we would never know whether or
not we were reading the truth.

CHAPTER XIII

Exit the Baroness

If Rostovsky's memoirs would make fascinating reading, those of Moura Budberg, had she written them, would have been rivetting. More than one well-known author has approached me in the hope that I could assist them write a full-length biography of her but too much remains unknown and she destroyed all her personal papers before she died. A unique personality in every way, she was of such importance to Russia that she appears to have been allowed to operate as a virtually independent agent of influence.

Although bureaucracy permeates every facet of the Soviet system and the lives of the myriads of people employed by the KGB, in the offices of the most influential men of Moscow's hierarchy, red tape is cut when it comes to advancing communism's aim of world domination if a new "tool" of major importance appears on the scene. Then departmentalism can go by the board.

Those working abroad for the Soviets in the higher political echelons may or may not be controlled directly by the KGB octopus. They may be the personal "eyes" for the chairman of the KGB himself or for the chief of one of the directorates. They may be working directly for the Politboro or even under the auspices of the Soviet leader himself—or a combination of any of these various possibilities.

Baroness Moura Budberg's exact relationship with Moscow has never been made clear. She knew Reilly from 1918 days just as she knew Peters, vice chairman of the Cheka at that time; she was totally involved with Maxim Gorki for a number of years and was on friendly terms with Stalin. She told me that she had met Reilly "several times" in the 1920s—clearly in Russia![1] On her own admission she had contacts with members of the Soviet Embassy in London, and Guy Burgess was a regular visitor to her flat in London before he fled into the shadows of the Kremlin's walls.

At the same time, I am convinced that she had a very genuine and deep affection for my father; and when he died in February 1970, she arranged for a special memorial service for him at the Russian Orthodox Church in London, which she alone attended in a solitary vigil. My family was angry but, in retrospect, I realize that she was expressing her love for him in her own very Russian manner.

The late Harold Nicholson declared that Moura Budberg was "the cleverest woman of her day in London." Certainly the actress Simone Signoret, when filming Chekov's *Seagull* with James Mason in 1969, which Moura had helped adapt for the screen, was largely wrong when she declared: "The old hag claims to be a baroness but we all suspect her of being an old Russian phony." "Phony," she may have been, but only in that most did not know of her Soviet connection.

If confirmation of Moura's first loyalty is necessary, it comes from a former senior officer of MI5 who informed me that there is no question in his mind but that the baroness was a Soviet agent and that he interrogated her on more than one occasion. The late Major Stephen Alley M.C., an MI5 officer since 1919, who had previously worked for SIS in Russia, had also voiced his doubts to me about Baroness Budberg many years earlier.

Moura had highly placed friends both sides of the Iron Curtain and, just as she was capable of loving more than one man at a time, so did the essentially Russian baroness enjoy life with her friends in England. But, as was the case with Reilly, when the chips were down, her first loyalty was to Russia—something Reilly himself had always known from the very first time he met her.

Her charm and intelligence drew many household names to the more or less open-house "salon" she held in the evenings. Somerset Maugham, Harold Nicholson, Anthony Eden, Alexander Korda—for whom she worked after the war as a personal assistant—the Duff Coopers, John Gielgud, Graham Greene, Arthur Koestler, Peter Ustinov, and Nöel Coward were among those who called on her to quaff vodka and indulge in political and literary talk. As already mentioned, Guy Burgess was a regular visitor at her flat. And, until their respective deaths, she regularly met with both H. G. Wells and my father. In his will, Wells left her some money together with an interest in some stocks which yielded almost nothing.

During the war Moura worked as a gofer for the Free French publication *France Libre*. It is not clear what relationship she was maintaining with Moscow at this time. I met her several times in the course of the war and from her conversation, it appeared that she was very much *au courant* with the affairs of the Soviet Embassy in London—yet without giving any secrets away.

After the Second World War, when relations between the Soviet Union and the West turned sour and went from bad to worse, the Baroness made a number of trips in and out of Moscow. She stood in good stead with Stalin and did sterling indirect propaganda work for the USSR, arranging for groups of Russian *artistes* to appear on the London stage to much acclaim. Once in the 1960s[2] she telephoned me while my father was ill to tell me she was going abroad for a month. I asked her where she was going. She replied: "Albania—for a holiday." That anybody from Britain should visit Albania, a country more Communist than any other and with virtually no diplomatic relations with the outside world, seemed extraordinary. How the Baroness persuaded Enver Hoxna to receive her I shall never know.

In 1974, she decided to leave England for good and settle in Italy—the land she had known so well in the 1920s when she had lived there with Gorki—and to be near her son who had moved there from the Isle of Wight, where he had been farming. She invited me to a farewell party in London a few days before she left for Italy, but most unfortunately, I had an important prior engagement; I was never to see her again. Perhaps she moved from London because she had a presentiment that her days were numbered: she died a few months later in November at the age of eighty-three.

Before her death, Moura destroyed all her personal papers and as with General Orlov, must have taken many secrets with her to the grave. Like Reilly himself, who had first spotted her potentialities, Baroness Budberg was a political adventuress with split loyalties. Like Reilly she had infinite charm and a passionate nature. More intellectual and more patient than he, she was a wonderful listener and gave the impression of being a great communicator, yet never gave anything away. She was, perhaps, the Soviet Union's most effective agent-of-influence ever to appear on London's political and intellectual stage.

CHAPTER XIV

The Enemy Within

The full extent of Sidney Reilly's "legacy," the widespread penetration of the United States and Britain—the USSR's allies during World War II—was to become devastatingly apparent not long after the G.I.'s, Tommies, and their families had been celebrating the end of hostilities, blissfully unaware that the Cold War, which is still with us today, was about to be declared.

For myself, I especially remember dining with my father at a well-known London restaurant shortly after the end of World War II. During the war he had been deputy undersecretary of state at the Foreign Office and director of the Political Warfare Executive responsible for "black" and "white" propaganda. He was a lifelong expert on Russia. There were two others at dinner that night: Sir Orme Sargent, who was head of the Foreign Office, and Jan Masaryk.[1] Throughout the meal there were lengthy and animated discussions not about consolidating peace, but about the tremendous danger the Soviet Union presented to the world, and the risks of another war.

All three agreed on a forecast, remarkable in view of the current changes going on in China, that if there were another war, it would be between Russia on the one side against the United States, Britain, and China. All three maintained that before the war was over, Roosevelt had set the stage for a further war by overriding Churchill at the "Big Three" con-

ferences and allowing Eisenhower to give away half of
Europe to Stalin. Churchill's "Iron Curtain" speech at Fulton, although an apposite warning, was a case of shutting
the stable door after the horse had bolted.

But, as was soon revealed, the Roosevelt administration,
including White House staff, was riddled with Soviet agents
and Communists. The NKVD had implemented with brilliant skills the advice consistently put forward by Reilly that
the most effective form of subversion was to place "agents-
of-influence" abroad in important posts where they could
not only be intelligence gatherers, but could also exert a
major influence on policy-making.

During the 1940s, the FBI did indeed keep an eye on a
number of Communists, including some in Government such
as Harry Dexter White;[2] but the knowledge that a veritable
regiment of Soviet agents existed in North America only
began to become apparent in September 1945, with the
defection from the Soviet embassy in Ottawa of cypher clerk
Igor Gouzenko. Astonishingly, Gouzenko nearly failed in
his efforts. Canadian Prime Minister Mackenzie King was
intent on cementing a strong friendship with the USSR and
at first issued an order that Gouzenko should be instructed
to return to the Soviet embassy the secret documents he had
stolen.

In the same year that Gouzenko defected, Elizabeth Bentley confessed to the FBI that she had taken over the running
of a spy ring following the death of NKVD agent Jacob
Golos, who had been her lover. She was able to identify a
number of senior government officials who had assisted her
in her espionage work. In addition to Harry Dexter White,
those named included Lauchlin Currie, a presidential aide
in the White House.

Elizabeth Bentley[3] testified before a grand jury that her
spy ring received secret and confidential reports from the
OSS, the State, Navy, and Army departments. At a U. S.
Senate Subcommittee hearing, Bentley said: "We knew what

was going on in the inner chambers of the U. S. Government up to and including the White House."

The Gouzenko defection led to lengthy, complex work (Code name: Operation Bride) in the breaking of Russian cyphers by cryptologists, and the Canadians were eventually, in 1950, able to pass on to Washington a long list of Soviet agents in the United States who had cooperated with the Canadian spy ring. In addition to "illegals," it was estimated that in 1950, out of 663 Communist diplomats in the U. S., 210 were Soviet agents, and that out of 383 officials from Communist countries employed at the United Nations, 165 were spies.[4]

The Canadians were amazed and dismayed at the size of the espionage system disclosed and at the number of people in key positions who were in NKVD employ. Atomic secrets, U. S. troop movements, and the planning of subversion in both Canada and Britain were the agents' target areas. Twenty-six people were discovered in the first spy ring, of whom ten were of foreign origin, ten Canadian-born, and six English-born. In less than forty-eight hours after Gouzenko had started his debriefing, thirteen members of Canadian Government departments were arrested. Thanks to the protective friendship of Lester Pearson, later Canadian premier, one Soviet agent of Canadian origin, Herbert Norman, temporarily escaped exposure. Norman, another Trinity College, Cambridge, "mole," went on to become Canadian ambassador to Japan, high commissioner in New Zealand, and ambassador in Egypt. Following questioning by the CIA in Cairo in 1957 he committed suicide. In a new book,[5] *No Sense of Evil, Espionage: The Case of Herbert Norman*, Professor James Barros produces evidence to show that Lester Pearson deliberately covered up for Norman and lied to the Canadian parliament. In the opinion of Barros, at the very least Pearson's behavior should have forfeited him any right to be Canada's foreign minister—let alone premier.

The NKVD *resident* in Ottawa was one Vitali Pavlov, posing as the embassy's second secretary while GRU agents operated under the military attaché, Colonel Nicolay Zabotin (code name Grant). Canadian traitors recruited by Zabotin's assistant, Major Rogov, and members of a spy ring known as "B Group" included Dernford Smith, Ned Mazerall, and Israel Halperin, professor of mathematics at Queens University. In addition, the Royal Canadian Air Force was found to have harbored a traitor in Squadron Leader Matt Nightingale.

As the result of a lead deduced from information provided by Gouzenko, it was established that Dr. Allan Nunn May, who had worked with the atomic research team in Canada, had given the Russians samples of U-285 uranium, and progress reports on the development of an atom bomb. Arrested in March 1946, Nunn May was given a ten-year sentence. On his release he became professor of physics in Ghana.

The West was subsequently shocked by the news that Dr. Klaus Fuchs, who had been working on the development of the atom bomb at Los Alamos in New Mexico, had been supplying the Soviets with scientific data since 1943. Eventually arrested in England in 1950 while employed at the British atomic station Harwell, he confessed to passing to the Russians details of atom bomb manufacture and other information on the current work being undertaken on the hydrogen bomb. He was sentenced to fourteen years' imprisonment and on release obtained a scientific post in East Germany. The NKVD had shown astonishing foresight in recruiting Fuchs, who admitted to having been a Communist since 1932.

It was about this time, too, that the controversial trial, conviction, and execution of Julius and Ethel Rosenberg occurred in America. They, also, had been charged with passing atomic secrets to the Russians. That the Rosenbergs were charged at all was mainly due to "Operation Bride," the breaking of the KGB codes at the time—a feature of the case which, for security reasons, could not be revealed in court.[6]

Bruno Pontecurvo was yet another atomic scientist who had been passing secrets to the Soviets. He had worked both in Canada and at Harwell but fled from England to Russia in 1950 before an MI5 net could close in on him. In Moscow, he became Comrade Bruno Maximovich Pontecorvo, at the Institute of Nuclear Physics.

Discoveries, confessions, and defections both to and from Russia followed with bewildering rapidity. The British Burgess and Maclean, tipped off by "Third Man" Philby,[7] fled to Moscow to avoid arrest. Maclean, as first secretary at the British embassy in Washington, was joint secretary to the Anglo-American Combined Policy Committee on nuclear developments and was able to keep the Soviets fully informed on both policy and technical developments in this area.

Maclean never received a penny from the Russians during his spying work, but once in Moscow he was posted as "an adviser" to the Foreign Ministry and later worked at the Institute of World Economy and International Relations. He had a dacha in the Foreign Ministry complex outside Moscow. In his obituary, following his death in 1984,[8] *Izvestia* described him as a man of "high moral qualities who for all his conscious life was devoted to the high ideals of Soviet progress, humanism, peace and international co-operation."

After Maclean and Burgess arrived in Moscow, the KGB established a special section of the Top Secret Archives department of the First (formerly Foreign) Directorate to deal solely with their material. One of those working in this section was Kislitsyn, former MVD cypher clerk at the Soviet embassy in London (1945–48) and assistant to Vladimir Petrov, the KGB *rezident* in Australia who defected to the West. Petrov who had served for twenty-one years in the KGB was able to confirm that it was a "Third Man" in Washington who had tipped off Burgess and Maclean.

Back in the United States, a second spy ring to that of Elizabeth Bentley in which Whittaker Chambers, a Communist since the 1920s but who broke with the Party in

1938, was a leading light, was made public in 1948. Chambers identified Alger Hiss, a senior official in the State Department, as a long-serving Soviet agent. This revelation and the trial of Alger Hiss that followed rocked America to its foundations.

At one point Secretary of State Dean Acheson felt he had to defend Hiss, and some senators and congressmen attacked the FBI as being a "sinister" organization. Yet Hiss, a proven Communist, was shown to have provided classified documents to the Soviet agent, Colonel Boris Bykov, head of GRU operations in the U.S.

During and following the investigation and trial of Hiss, on whom the FBI had adverse reports dating back to 1939 but whom they did not interrogate until 1948, Harry Dexter White[9] was also being accused of espionage. He dropped down dead three days later. In addition, Marvin Smith, a Justice department friend of Hiss, was pushed, fell, or jumped to his death down a stairwell, Lawrence Duggan of the State department and another friend of Hiss was pushed, fell, or jumped to his death; the life of Harvard Professor F. O. Mathieson, wanted for questioning about his Communist connections, ended when he was pushed, jumped, or fell out of a Boston hotel window. At later dates, and for different reasons, Jan Masaryk and the Canadian traitor Herbert Norman also departed from this world via windows.

The long arm of coincidence? Perhaps, but "falling out of windows" is an excellent murder-method for the assassin who wishes to shut someone's mouth permanently and leave the cause of death in doubt.

Meanwhile, FBI and CIA interest had been growing in an organization established before the war known as IPR (Institute of Pacific Relations). This was an international grouping of "Institutes" with a headquarters secretariat in New York, to which the periodicals *Amerasia* and *Pacific Affairs* were related.

Official interest in IPR was first taken in January 1941 when the chief of the FBI in San Francisco received instructions to obtain and forward certain IPR literature. In about November 1941 an active investigation was instituted.

In February 1945, an OSS official read in an issue of *Amerasia* a direct quotation of his which had been included in a highly classified memorandum. The director of the OSS security office, Frank Bielaski, found that several people connected with *Amerasia* also had IPR connections.

At midnight on March 11th, 1945, Bielaski, heading up a team of four, surreptitiously broke into the *Amerasia* offices and seized numerous U. S. Government classified documents.

As a result, the FBI was asked to make an investigation under the espionage statutes. Six people were ultimately charged, but because of the manner in which the evidence had been obtained two defendants only—Philip Jaffe, the then editor of *Amerasia*, and Emmanuel Larsen—were merely fined $2,500 and $500 respectively. The others who included a member of the State Department and one from U. S. Naval Intelligence, after entering *nolo contendere* pleas, got off scot-free.

However, following the various disclosures of widespread Soviet espionage in the United States, further investigations into IPR were instituted in 1951, and congressional hearings into IPR before the U. S. Senate Internal Security Subcommittee lasted eleven months, from July 25, 1951, to June 20, 1952. The printed transcript of the hearings ran to over 5,000 pages, some 20,000 documents were examined and testimony taken from 66 witnesses. U. S. intelligence circles have described the IPR investigations as "comprehensive, meticulous and masterly."

IPR was shown to provide an umbrella for Soviet agents employed not only in gathering political and military intelligence but also in disseminating covert and subversive propaganda. It was described in the Report of the hearings as being like a "specialized political flypaper in its attractive power for Communists."

Fourteen individuals directly connected with IPR refused

to answer questions on the grounds of self-incrimination, nineteen others who, according to the published Report of the Hearings (Appendix V), "were by evidence involved in subversive activity" were out of the country or otherwise unavailable for subpoena. Among the nineteen was one Michael Greenberg who, according to the Report, "collaborated with agents of the Soviet intelligence apparatus as shown by sworn testimony" and was "affiliated with *Amerasia*." Among others listed as having been directly associated with Soviet military intelligence were Alger Hiss of the State department, Lauchlin Currie, an aide to the president, and Owen Lattimore, Greenberg's predecessor as editor of *Pacific Affairs*, an IPR publication.

Two Russian defectors, Bogolepov and Barmine, testified that IPR was a covert organization for Soviet military intelligence.

Michael Greenberg, who was of British nationality—as was Lattimore—and had been an undergraduate at Cambridge, after leaving the IPR conglomerate had been appointed to the U. S. Board of Economic Warfare in November 1942, and shared an office with Lauchlin Currie[10] in the White House. The Report of the IPR Congressional Hearings states that the Soviet spy Elizabeth Bentley testified to Greenberg being "a Communist in the IPR cell when she recruited him for espionage work in Washington." Professor George Taylor of Washington testified that Greenberg was so blatant in his beliefs that he was shocked when Greenberg obtained a White House post. So much for wartime security in the White House where, according to the Report, there was only one man "in charge of the so-called security."

In July 1944, Greenberg was transferred to the Foreign Economic Administration and to the Department of State in September 1945. In June, 1946, he was let go following a reduction in personnel and, according to the same Congress report "he was barred from competing in civil service examinations on March 7, 1947 because of his questionable loyalty."

At the time of the Senate Internal Security Subcommittee hearings, Greenberg's whereabouts were unknown. He was believed to have been in Switzerland, but his last known address was recorded in the report of the hearings as being "Trinity College, Cambridge"[11]—perhaps Cambridge's most respected College, but one whose products had included Philby, Blunt, Burgess, the American Michael Straight, and the self-confessed Soviet agent Leo Long.

When I was in Washington in early 1985, Michael Straight confided in me that Greenberg had been in the same Communist "cell" with him at Cambridge in the 1930s. Having lost touch with Greenberg after coming down from University, Straight was surprised to run into him one day during the war in a Washington street. On being asked what he was doing in Washington, Greenberg replied that he was working for the State Department. Michael Straight was astonished, but the truth of Greenberg's statement was confirmed to him by his Cambridge friends. Later Straight noticed Greenberg's name in the press as being connected with *Amerasia* prior to the latter's Governmental positions.

A bizarre sequel to this arose out of Michael Straight's book *After Long Silence*, published in 1983, in which he refers to his Soviet contact as going under the code name "Michael Green."[12] Learning of this, Michael Greenberg, through his London lawyer Geoffrey Bindman, threatened to sue Straight for libel as he had changed his name from Greenberg to Green.[13] A strange coincidence, but no legal action followed as quite clearly the Soviet "Michael Green" and Michael Greenberg were two different people. Yet equally clearly Michael Greenberg/Green had beeen shown to have been in his time another Cambridge communist.

Recent efforts of mine to discuss with Greenberg the former Cambridge man's wartime role in Washington proved unsuccessful. While contending that I appeared to be relying on McCarthyite sources, he declined the proffered opportunity to set the record straight by providing answers to my questions either in writing or at an interview.

The internal danger to the Western democratic way of life lies not only in the presence in our midst of KGB agents but perhaps even more from the harboring of "fellow travelers." The report of the British privy councillors on security states: "Once the main risk to be guarded against was espionage by foreign powers carried out by professional agents. Today the chief risks are presented by Communists. This risk extends to sympathisers with Communism." Similar commissions in Australia and Canada reached the same conclusions.

The U. S. Senate Judiciary's Subcommittee for Internal Security and Terrorism was disbanded by Senator Edward Kennedy during the Carter regime but re-established under Senator Admiral Denton with the advent to power of President Reagan. At the time, James Angleton, the former chief of CIA counter-intelligence wrote: "The Senate's revival of a subcommittee charged with exposing the apparatus of espionage, subversion and terrorism inside our shores promises a long overdue restoration of the congressional world over the enemies within."

It must be admitted, nevertheless, that in the United States recently, the lure of dollars—so dominant in the American way of life—offered by Soviet agents, as opposed to ideological convictions, has led to the betrayal of secrets to Moscow.

The objectives of Mikhail Gorbachev and his Kremlin associates remain the same as those of Lenin and Stalin: a Communist world dominated and controlled from Moscow and one in which democracy, as we understand it, has no place. The wiles originally generated by Dzerzhinsky and Reilly subsequently enabled the Soviets to recruit agents for the NKVD—a forerunner of the KGB—from among the intellectuals and middle classes in U. S. and Canadian governmental circles as well as some of the brightest brains in British universities. These traitors who became the "enemy within" believed Maxim Gorki when he wrote in "To American Intellectuals," published in 1932:

> The theory of Marx and Lenin is the highest pinnacle yet reached by scientific thought honestly investigating all social phenomena."

This form of propaganda and that which accompanied the Russian Revolution blinded not only the Russian people, but also much of the rest of the world to the ghastly excesses carried out by the Cheka butchers, and to the orgy of terror instituted by Stalin during which more Russians met their death than in the course of three revolutions and a civil war.

Today, Soviet propaganda is equally insidious, employs highly sophisticated techniques, and is backed by enormous funds, estimated by the CIA in 1980 at over $3 billion per annum. Newspapers, periodicals, and 'black' radio stations are backed by forged documents,[14] "planted" articles, rumor-spreading, and disinformation. Millions of dollars are spent on "front" peace, antinuclear, quasireligious, and trade union organizations in addition to funding Communist parties in other countries, some of whose card-carrying members are from time to time instructed to resign their membership and go underground for covert work.

Criticism of Soviet activities abroad is dismissed as "mere anti-Soviet slander." One of the most successful and influential counters to anti-Communism has been the well-known Kahn and Sayers book *The Great Conspiracy*. Translated into numerous languages, it has been sold in some thirty different countries.[15]

One wonders what Reilly would think, were he alive today, of the present monster KGB machine which he was instrumental in fostering in its infancy; a machine where regular intelligence, counter-intelligence and propaganda work form only part of its activites. Hand in hand with these go subversion, kidnapping, murder, torture and terrorism.[16] The number of people employed by the KGB is

not known: I have seen estimates as low as 250,000, and
of over 4,000,000. The original forerunner of the KGB
was the Okhrana,[17] founded by Peter the Great in 1697,
and for generations murder and torture have been among
the main tools of the Okhrana's various successors. In the
heady days of 1918, the September issue of *The Cheka
Bulletin* complained bitterly that my father, arrested for
his part in the "Lockhart Plot" while Reilly escaped, had
been released from prison instead of being submitted to
torture:

> Why wasn't Lockhart subjected to the most refined tor-
> tures, in order to get information and addresses, of which
> such a bird must have had many? Tortures, the mere
> description of which would have instilled a cold terror?

In the free world, most people are aware that the KGB
is a dangerous animal; but few know how really dangerous,
and the extent to which its tentacles spread into every sphere
of human activity. Who knows how many thousands of
Soviet directed agents permeate the West and how many are
active in the developing countries? The illegal crossing of
frontiers or entry by sea into foreign countries is child's
play—as witness the many thousands of illegal immigrants
from Mexico into California, the traffic of Pakistanis into
England, and the illegal movements of drug traffickers and
other criminals. How much easier it must be for a highly
trained KGB operator!

Soviet embassies, consulates, and Soviet and satellite
delegations to the United Nations are well-known stamping
grounds for KGB and GRU agents. A number of other
agents succeed in entering the West in the guise of dissidents
or defectors. Cyril Ghenkin, former member of the KGB's
Fourth Directorate and one time aide to the Soviet master
spy Rudolf Abel, who defected in 1973 and with whom I
have discussed the problem of Russian infiltration of the
West, maintains that the Soviets have no need to invade us

as they are already here, building up with infinite patience to take over from inside.[18]

A Tass communiqué of December 1975, reported the formation of a Soviet Society called "Rodina" (My Fatherland) to which all Russians outside Russia—"Whites," defectors, dissidents, and others of all or no political persuasions, are deemed to belong automatically as "fellow countrymen abroad."

Drugs are another weapon in the KGB armory. The finest and most powerful heroin emanates from East Germany and is marketed in West Germany, where the West German police estimate that the U. S. armed forces account for no less than sixty-five percent of its consumption and at a price one-thirtieth of that obtaining in the streets of New York.

Although the Freedom of Information Act is clearly a real safeguard of the American constitution and of civil liberty, it has not made the battle against the "enemy within" any easier, and eventually led FBI chief Judge Webster to remark in 1978 that the Bureau was "practically out of the domestic security field."

Pressure from the Senate's Subcommittee on Security and Terrorism in 1984 persuaded the Justice Department to amend the restrictive guidelines to the FBI, issued by Attorney General Levi; but there are still some loopholes which the KGB can exploit in order to continue to develop their "enemy within" strategy.

McCarthyism certainly took the witch-hunting for Communists much too far. Yet, ironically, when McCarthy died in 1957, a broken man, he was unaware that the State Department security chief had submitted a report to his superiors naming hundreds of security risks. [Leading members of the U. S. intelligence community have also told me of their belief that the later witch-hunts against the CIA and FBI by Senator Frank Church of Idaho and New York Congressman Pike probably contributed more damage to the United States than anything perpetrated by Senator McCarthy.]

Today, the FBI spends some $14,000,000 per year and employs some 400 clerks solely on vetting files and documents for availability to the public. Top class agents should really be assigned to this work, but there are not enough of them to go round, and inevitably some vital secrets leak out. For instance, a clerk vetting a document someone has asked to see under the F.O.I. Act may black out the name of a secret agent named in the document; but it may well turn out that the agent is "blown" because the number plate of his car may be mentioned on another page—not blacked out. The cloak of anonymity is the correct uniform for an intelligence officer.

While excesses in zeal by Western intelligence agencies must not be countenanced, it is the duty of governments and the citizens of all freedom loving nations not to impede the fight against the "enemy within." That enemy is controlled by "the enemy without"—the world's most efficient and active intelligence organization, partly spawned by Reilly, and one which does not hesitate to pluck the brightest fourteen and fifteen year old children from Soviet schools and give them ten years intensive training preparatory to them joining the KGB.

CHAPTER XV

Counter-Action

The effectiveness of U. S. and British counter-intelligence during the inter-war period in so far as it was targeted against the USSR and communist subversion was minimal and without exaggeration could well be described as lamentable. Yet, to a great extent this was understandable. Germany had been the enemy in World War I, and the threat of a communist-dominated world directed from the newly born Soviet state was scarcely recognized. Russia had been financially and physically decimated and by the 1930s, it was Hitler and Nazi Germany with which the intelligence world was preoccupied.

In Britain, counter-intelligence was handled by MI5, an organization originally under War Office control, which achieved effective independence in 1916 with direct access to the prime minister. Throughout the First World War and until he reached the age of sixty in 1939, Colonel Kell—later Major General Sir Vernon Kell—had been MI5's director with Eric Wilson as his chief of staff until 1935.

MI5 had proved itself an efficient unit in operations against German spies during the 1914–18 War but, come the end of the war, its effectiveness was greatly impaired. Along with the armed forces, MI5's budget was drastically curtailed. In 1918, MI5 had some eight hundred personnel; by the 1930's the staff in its London headquarters in Cromwell Road numbered less than thirty[1]—and this in-

cluded secretaries. One of its brighter younger men during
the interwar period was Guy Liddel, whom Kell had recruited in the 1920s from Scotland Yard's Special Branch,
and who was later to become deputy director of MI5. It
was not long after joining MI5 that Liddell's suspicions
were aroused that Reilly might be a double agent, but
there was no tangible proof. Reilly's SIS chief, Captain
Sir Mansfield Cumming R.N., had had similar doubts from
time to time, as had the American intelligence agent Kalamatiano in 1918.

Reilly knew almost as much about MI5's activities as
those who worked in the service: one of his best friends
was the MI5 officer, Major Stephen Alley, M.C.[2] whom
Reilly had known since 1918. The "Ace of Spies" was also
on intimate terms in the 1920s with Sir Basil Thompson,
the Head of Scotland Yard's Special Branch, who worked
closely with Kell. On reaching Russia in 1925, Sidney Reilly
was clearly in a position to reveal to Dzerzhinsky a great
deal of the inner workings of MI5.

As for the United States, although the U. S. Army
and Navy handled their own security matters, counter-
intelligence as we know it today was non-existent until early
1934. It was then that Franklin D. Roosevelt and Attorney
General Homer S. Cummings gave FBI chief J. Edgar Hoover secret instructions to investigate Nazi elements in America and any anti-American or anti-Jewish activities. The
subsequent investigation was inconsequential: Hoover did
not have sufficient personnel available who were equipped
for this type of work.

A few months later, on 24th August, 1934, Hoover
received a further directive from Roosevelt. It was to
investigate subversive activities, *including communism*, and
to liaise in this area with Naval and Military Intelligence;
but Hoover pointed out once again that the FBI did not
have the officers to handle such investigations competently.

As a result, Attorney General Homer Cummings gave
instructions on September 10th, 1934, that all forty-five FBI

Field Officers were to be responsible for the new investigative duties. To assist them fifty new officers were to be allocated for full time work in the sphere of subversion; one for each Field Officer and five for work at FBI headquarters. At this time the Bureau employed five hundred people; it was officially subordinate to the Department of Justice, as it still is today.

Hoover, former special assistant to the Attorney General, had been appointed director of the FBI in May 1924, at the age of twenty-nine, and was to remain its chief for nearly fifty years—an astonishing length of time for anyone to survive through the powerbase infighting which is the norm in political Washington. The new directives led to Hoover's men uncovering a number of Nazi and Japanese spies but, although Hoover had considered communism to be an international conspiracy ever since the Russian Revolution, the evidence turned up about communist subversion was of relatively minor importance.

Prior to these various new directives, FBI activities had been almost entirely restricted to crime. The "Bureau of Investigation," as the FBI was first called, was established in July 1908, towards the end of Theodore Roosevelt's second term, and its first chief, Stanley W. Finch, was charged with the duty of investigating political and big business corruption. The Bureau was assisted in its work by volunteers from the American Protective League which, by 1924, had swollen to some 250,000 members.

In 1924, there was a major change in the Bureau's guidelines. Harlan Fiske Stone, Calvin Coolidge's Attorney General, ordered the Bureau to cease its activities in the political sphere and to confine itself to dealing with law breaking. The American Protective League volunteers were dispensed with. The age of the G-Man[3] had arrived.

Although communism had spawned an embryo political entity in the United States in 1919,[4] following the formation of the Third International (Comintern), it was not considered by most people to be a potentially major danger, although

Russian-inspired and Moscow-dominated. After the Russian Revolution, had not Woodrow Wilson sent a message to the Soviet Congress expressing the sympathy of the American people for the Russian people in their struggle for freedom? Had he not pressured the British, who had arrested Trotsky early in 1917, into releasing him so that he could join forces with Lenin in Russia? Had he not always been half-hearted over "intervention"?

With the storm clouds of World War II looming ever closer, further changes in the FBI's functions were to emerge. On June 29th, 1939, Roosevelt issued secret instructions that the FBI was to control all espionage,[5] counter-espionage and counter-sabotage activities in liaison with Military and Naval Intelligence.[6]

On September 6th, 1939, following the outbreak of war in Europe, the President's June instructions to the FBI were confirmed publicly and the Bureau expanded during the war to an eight thousand strong body. Some fifty new agents per week were taken on.

Despite this swift growth, until the case of FBI agent Robert Miller, charged with betraying secrets to the Russian agent, Svetlana Ogorodmikov, there has been no known case of a traitor or "mole"[7] within the FBI camp. Each new agent was given a thorough positive vetting—from "womb to tomb," as they say.

Throughout World War II, American and British counter-intelligence was naturally concentrated against German and Japanese agents with considerable success—especially by MI5. The Soviet Union became an ally and although an increasingly watchful eye was maintained on Communist activities in the United States and in Britain, it was not nearly watchful enough.

From the 1930s onwards, the Soviet secret agencies recruited to the Communist cause members of the elite in all spheres of influence. In the process, and despite periodic decimation by Stalin of its own hierarchy, the GPU/NKVD was molded into an organization which the British traitor from MI6, Kim Philby was to describe as "an elite force." The GPU/NKVD had indeed heeded Reilly's advice that the most important and rewarding results were to be obtained by placing or enlisting agents in positions of influence.

In 1950, the U.S. Congress passed the Internal Security Act that barred all aliens,[8] irrespective of status, where entry would endanger public safety. It was more of a political gesture than anything else: as a deterrent to wily Soviet agents, it had little effect. Moreover, communists with diplomatic status could continue to be admitted to the United States. As J. Edgar Hoover was to remark in the same year:

"Experience has revealed that foreign espionage agents seek the protection of a legal cover. By that I mean they seek admittance into the U. S. on diplomatic passports. To further avert suspicion, a high ranking espionage agent may very well be employed as a clerk or in some minor capacity in a foreign establishment."

The free world was to pay and continues to pay for its lack of awareness of the way in which Reilly, "The First Man" of a Western intelligence service to defect to the Soviets, had been able to signpost the road whereby Soviet secret agencies could help Russia to pursue its aim of a communist world dominated by Moscow.

Although the intelligence services on both sides of the Atlantic were much occupied with the question of Kim Philby's loyalty or disloyalty, the late 1950s appear to have been something of a close season for spy-catching. The exposure of the Rudolf Abel spy ring in 1957 was one exception; Abel, a KGB colonel, was one of the shrewdest of Soviet "illegals" and had entered the United States in 1948. He had joined the GPU as early as 1927, and ironically, had received part of his training from Orlov.

Rudolf Abel set up his "spy-shop" in Fulton Street, Brooklyn as Emil Goldfus, photographer. A competent performer, like Rostovsky, on the guitar and a passable painter, Abel fitted well into the generally bohemian area near Brooklyn Heights. Hidden in his studio was almost undetectable radio equipment, and for nine years he carried out his espionage undisturbed, only to be given away eventually by his rather alcoholic assistant Reino Hayhanen. The Colonel spoke perfect English; he had been born in Newcastle-on-Tyne, England as Willie Fischer, off-spring of a German father and a Russian mother. After his arrest and interrogation in June 1957, he claimed to have refused an offer of $10,000 from the FBI to "turn" and work for them.

Sentenced in 1957 to thirty years imprisonment, Abel was exchanged in Berlin at Checkpoint Charlie in February, 1962, for U-2 pilot Gary Powers, who had been shot down over Russia in 1960.[9] On his return to Russia, Abel was rewarded with a handsome dacha outside Moscow, a car and chauffeur and kept supplied with his favorite American cigarettes.

It was on Wednesday, January 23, 1963, that Philby finally left the free world to join his fellow traitors in Moscow; the story of his defection has been well chronicled. MI6 and MI5 and the Americans were completely aghast that such a senior intelligence officer who, while working all the while for MI6—including a period in Washington in liaison with the CIA—and a man who had even been tipped by some as a future head of MI6, had been a KGB agent all the time. That he had headed the section spying against the Soviets was all grist to the KGB mill.

Whereas Rostovsky and the NKVD appear to have concentrated most of their attentions on Cambridge, Oxford, was not entirely neglected. Jenifer Fischer-Williams, later Mrs. Hart, who joined the Communist Party in 1935, was an Oxford student whom the Soviets had intended to use as a "mole" when she obtained a post in the Home Office. She met with more than one Soviet "control" in London's Kew Gardens, in the belief that she was merely helping the Communist party, but severed all connections when the Russo-Nazi pact was announced.

After Burgess and Maclean had fled to Russia and Philby had been cleared of the charge of being "The Third Man," Igor Gouzenko was again questioned about Soviet espionage in Britain before he defected. Gouzenko is reported to have said: "There is not the slightest doubt in my mind that there was a Soviet agent inside MI5 during the period 1942–1943 and possibly later on." He claimed to have learnt this from a Lieutenant Liubimov, a comrade of his from the Moscow Intelligence Directorate in the Cypher Department in Ottawa. There have been various opinions about who this spy might have been. Chapman Pincher has made a strong case,[10] but one built almost entirely on circumstantial evidence, that it was Sir Roger Hollis, the head of MI5; others think that Gouzenko was probably referring to Anthony Blunt.

In the early 1960s, following a lead supplied by a Soviet defector, MI5 in Britain was able to round up a spy network operating in the naval field which came to be known as the "Portland spy ring." Heading this up was Gordon Lonsdale, his assistants Peter and Helen Kruger, also known as Morris and Lona Cohen, and Harold Houghton, and his girl friend Ethel Gee.

Lonsdale, the first Soviet national to be sentenced in Britain for espionage, spent little time in jail. Sent to prison in 1963, he was swapped for Greville Wynne on April 22nd, 1964 at Berlin's Checkpoint Heerstrasse. Lonsdale, whose real name was Konon Trofimovich Molody, wrote[11] subsequently in Russia under the pseudonym Georgiy Lonov, describing his work for the KGB from his early days as a student at London University where he "penetrated" a group of foreign students who were supposedly staff members of intelligence and counter-intelligence services of anti-Communist countries.

The traitor George Blake—another Cambridge product—who had joined MI6 in 1947, revealed to the Russians the identities of many British agents in Europe, and although sentenced in 1961 to no less than forty-two years in prison, did not spend very long behind bars. The KGB, with the aid of the criminal underworld, looked after its own and engineered his escape in 1966.

One MI5 success of the early 1960s was the nailing of John Vassall, a civilian employee of the Admiralty who had worked in the Naval Attaché's office in Moscow. Those who knew him said he was such an obvious homosexual, it was astonishing that he could be posted to such an intelligence sensitive post as Moscow. Sure enough, Vassall was inveigled by the KGB into homosexual parties, photographed and blackmailed into spying. Vassall was sentenced to eighteen years imprisonment in 1962.

More recently, MI5 officer Michael Bettany was caught trying to pass secrets from MI5's files to Arkadi Gouk, the First Secretary at London's Soviet Embassy. Following Bettaney's arrest and trial in April, 1984, Gouk, a top KGB officer in Britain since 1982, was deemed persona non grata by the Foreign Office and returned hurriedly to Moscow. Four days later Dennis Skinner, for fifteen years the Midland Bank's man in Moscow, married to a Russian and generally believed to have been a double agent, fell eleven floors to his death from his Moscow flat—one of the most popular ways the Soviet terror *apparat* has had of ridding itself of enemies or potential "squealers"—after appealing to the British Embassy for help.

In California in July 1985, Svetlana Ogorodmikov was caught and sentenced to eighteen years in jail for espionage while her husband received an eight year sentence. Ogorodmikov, among other things, was alleged to have seduced FBI agent Robert Miller. Miller's trial was the first in which an FBI officer has been convicted of espionage.

Perhaps more serious still are the implications of the discovery of the alleged spy ring in the U. S. Navy operated by members of the Walker family. And, even more serious, the revelation that vital secret information was being leaked to the Russians from the GCHQ[12] out-station listening post in Cyprus. Seven positively-vetted members of the station were alleged to have been black-mailed into giving Cyprus-based KGB agent Vladimir Semichastny some 1,300 secret documents, following homosexual orgies with an Arab which were photographed by the KGB. After a multimillion-pound trial at the Old Bailey lasting four months, nearly all in camera, the longest, largest most secret and most costly spy trial ever held in Britain—all seven men were acquitted. Nevertheless, both GCHQ and NSA in the United States are totally satisfied that top secret information of major importance reached Moscow from the Cyprus station.

Government Communications Headquarters (GCHQ) is the successor to the British "Government Code and Cypher School" which was founded in the early 1920s and is itself the successor to the brilliant cipher-breaking team of the Admiralty's Naval Intelligence Division under Admiral Sir Reginald ("Blinker") Hall. It was the breaking of German and Japanese ciphers which enabled the British to give advance warnings to Stalin about Hitler's invasion of Russia and to Roosevelt over Japan's intention in the Pacific; but the warnings went unheeded.

The National Security Agency (NSA) is the American counterpart to GCHQ and both organizations work together very closely. The NSA was founded by President Truman in 1952 by secret directive and for many years its very existence was denied; the initials were laughingly said to stand for "No Such Agency." NSA headquarters are at Fort G. Meade, twenty miles out of Washington.

Today, signals intelligence or "Sigint" is one of the most important weapons in the espionage war, the Americans alone employing some 120,000 people in this area; Russian infiltration into Allied Sigint is one of the KGB's principal tasks. The first major Soviet penetration of GCHQ Cheltenham to be revealed to the public was that of Geoffrey Prime, a GCHQ Soviet specialist, who admitted to spying for Moscow for fourteen years. He was jailed for thirty-eight years. At the conclusion of his trial, the Lord Chief Justice said that Prime had done "incalculable harm to the interests of security of the country and its friends." But James Bamford, a U. S. intelligence specialist, in his book *The Puzzle Palace*, has written: "As weak as security was at GCHQ, it was a fortress compared to NSA. The NSA was simply better at hiding how much and how badly it had been penetrated."

More often than not, whenever a KGB penetration of Western intelligence is discovered, there are attacks on the counter-intelligence services both in the media and behind the scenes in the intelligence services' own dark world. Counter-intelligence in bringing to book spies requires not only skill, concentration and aptitude for the work, but endless patience. It is usually a thankless task but arguably more important than intelligence gathering.

Ranking alongside Sigint in importance is the intelligence harvested from defectors. Since Reilly—"The First Man"[13] to defect—the number of defectors both to and from East and West has been gradually increasing, until now there would appear to be a steady stream in both directions. 1985 might well be termed "The Year of the Defector" with hardly a week passing without news of some defection. Undoubtedly, the most extraordinary tale is that of the double defector, Vitaly Yurchenko. One of the KGB's top men, Yurchenko defected in Rome in August 1985, to provide the CIA with priceless information, only to redefect a few months later back into the arms of the KGB with a tale of having been drugged and kidnapped by the Americans. It was information from Yurchenko that led to the exposure of Ronald Pelton as a spy within NSA. The suggestion made in some quarters that he was a "plant" to learn about U. S. policy intentions for the Reagan-Gorbachev summit meeting in Geneva are too far-fetched. In all probability, Yurchenko missed his wife and family and had second thoughts about living in the West.

Undoubtedly there are many more members of the KGB who would like to defect than actually do so. Understandably they are reluctant to leave their families and fear the consequences that might befall their families were they to defect.

CHAPTER XVI

Sidney Reilly:
Patriot or Traitor?

More and more of the world's intelligence services and students of intelligence history—particularly those in the United States—have come to learn that today's Soviet intelligence activities have matured to their present peak of efficiency through refinements of older techniques which they had developed in the late 1920s and during the 1930s. This was primarily achieved through learning, adapting and improving British espionage methods, then considered to be the best in the world, despite the drastic cuts made in the British Secret Service after the 1914–1918 War. Then, too, was the recruiting of "traitors within the gate" strategy conceived. And it was none other than Sidney Reilly who provided the Russians with the information, leads and many ideas which gave birth to a re-vamped organization which grew to become, in Philby's words, an "elite force"—the KGB. If Dzerzhinsky was the founding father of modern Soviet intelligence, Reilly was a fundamental element— perhaps the most important—in its incubation.

Within a matter of months of Reilly's return to Russia, sixty years ago, the Soviets began planning the implementation of his strategy for the conversion, subversion and perversion to the Communist cause of agents-of-influence such as the young men of Cambridge, Ottawa, New York, and Washington, who could be manipulated by the likes of Rostovsky. Recruitment of "eyes and ears" such as Moura

Budberg, with entree to leading political and intellectual circles, along with men of finely tuned brains such as Alexander Orlov, were but extensions of the same policy.

Since those days, the influence of the KGB has grown enormously. From Tokyo to Berlin and from Stockholm to Santiago, no corner of the globe, no sphere of government— including intelligence services—science, industry, political parties, and trade unions escapes Soviet attention and penetration.

Today, the number of traitors in the democracies caught spying for the Soviet Union appears to be on the increase— particularly in the United States. The counter-intelligence services to the West must be ever more watchful—as indeed should be every loyal citizen.

What is it that turns a man into a traitor, or "defector in situ" as I prefer to call such men as Burgess and MacLean? Was Reilly, who was indirectly responsible for recruiting so many such defectors in situ, a traitor himself? And, if so, to which country?

There are a number of reasons for such defections: the principal one is probably the lure of money offered by the KGB; the straightforward appeal to the naive of Communist ideology is another inducement to spy, although less so than it used to be. Disillusionment with U. S. society through knowledge of amorality in the corridors of power in governmental and intelligence circles is another motivation to betray secrets. Blackmail, particularly over sexual matters, is yet another.

One important reason for a man to turn spy, according to Admiral Stansfield Turner[1], former CIA director, is what he terms "psychological fulfillment" and a "need to find excitement or a sense of power and control." As an example, he cites Sidney Reilly, whom he describes as "a man who sold himself to various governments and clearly gained satisfaction not only from making money but from manipulating people and governments as well."

It is true that in a letter to my father, to which I have

already drawn attention, Reilly seems to have been greatly
attracted to Communist ideology when he wrote:

> It is bound by a process of evolution to conquer the world,
> as Christianity and the ideas of the French Revolution
> have done before it, and that nothing can stem its ever
> rising tide ... (Bolshevism) is the nearest approach, I
> know of, to a real democracy based upon true social
> justice and that may be destined to lead the world to the
> highest level of statesmanship—Internationalism.

Yet nothing in Reilly's life would seem to indicate that
he was attached to any ideology, except perhaps one of his
own devising—the core of which was Reilly himself. On
the other hand, his life was so full of contradictions, and
his attitudes at different times puzzled so many, that he may
have kept his most innermost thoughts to himself. In his
time, he had carried out great feats of espionage for Britain,
had worked for the Japanese, and for Russia under both the
Tsarist and the Communist regimes. He has been acclaimed
as a master spy by many and in many countries and "Ace
of Spies" he certainly was. But traitor or patriot? I wonder.
Perhaps, Russia—his country of birth—claimed his heart
and true loyalty in the end, but I am more inclined to think
of him as a professional spy whose ultimate loyalty lay only
and always to himself and, complex character that he was,
he worked primarily for what Stansfield Turner has called
"psychological fulfillment."

In the long history of espionage, I doubt if there has ever
been such an unusual master of his craft as Reilly, and I
doubt there will ever be another one again. As I also doubt
whether any authoritative accounts of his later life will be
released from the Soviet Union—records have almost certainly been destroyed—neither our children nor our children's children are ever likely to learn the true story of
Sigmund Rosenblum, alias Sidney Reilly and many other
names, in its totality.

Appendix I.

Extract from letter from Sidney Reilly to the author's father

Savoy Hotel, London.

November 24th

My Dear Lockhart,

My very short stay here has not given me as many opportunities as I would have liked for discussing with you the subject in which we are both so interested, namely the Russian Question. ....

The term "Bolshevism" has been applied so promiscuously that for the purpose of this letter, I find it expedient to define more clearly the sense in which I am using it:

I am not concerned at the moment with Bolshevism as a Super-Marxism, as a system for the social reconstruction of the world. I believe that in-so-far as this system contains practical and constructive ideas for the establishment of a higher social justice, it is bound by a process of evolution to conquer the world, as Christianity and the ideas of the French Revolution have done before it, and that nothing-least of all violent reactionary forces - can stem & its ever-rising tide. Incidentally I should also like to state here, that the much decried and so little understood "Soviets" which are the outward expression of Bolshevism as applied to pratical government, are the nearest approach, I know of, to a _real_ democracy based upon true social justice and that they may be destined to lead the world to the highest ideal of statemanship - Internationalism.

....

Believe me, my dear Lockhart,

Yours very sincerely,

Sidney Reilly

SIDNEY. G. REILLY.

Appendix II

Translation of letter sent to Sidney Reilly by Boris Savinkov from the Lubianka

October 7th 1924
Inner Prison
MOSCOW

My dear friend Sidney,

I have been given the possibility of writing to you and I am glad of it. I fear that neither Filossofov[1] nor my sister have forwarded to you my letters as I asked them. You are one of the few people whom I not only love but whose opinion I value. Permit me therefore to tell you everything as it has been.

Filossofov has written an article in *For Freedom*. Such an article I could not possibly expect from him. It does not matter that in his imagination, I am no more than a "dead dog"; and the Derenthals[2] either scoundrels or cowards. If that is the way he thinks about us, where were his eyes for several years? The point is that he asserts that I came to an agreement with the Bolsheviks beforehand in Paris; that I deceived him and all the others; that I took part in the "staging" of my trial and that I have gone through nothing more than an "amusing and silly farce." He also claims that I am endeavouring to "entice" him to Russia and that I am sitting at present not in prison but under the name of Reiss

1. Friend of Savinkov and Editor of Russian daily *For Freedom*, published in Warsaw.
2. Mr. and Mrs. Derenthal accompanied Savinkov to Russia. Derenthal was his secretary.

in the Savoy Hotel in Moscow. It is well that he abstained from the assertion that I have been an "informer" during my interrogation.

How shall I reply to this? That I am not a "camel"? ... I shall not disguise from you that, used as I am to being maligned, Filossofov's article left a deep scar, considering that apart from you and my sister, I was also thinking of him when I was awaiting my execution.

The truth is as follows: during my arrest (I was arrested in Minsk immediately after crossing the frontier), and afterwards during the interrogation, it became clear to me that:

(i) A.P.[3] is a member of the Communist Party; E[4] is a scoundrel; S.E.[5] has been working a long time with the Bolsheviks and that there does not exist any ghost of an organisation.
(ii) the active bands of "Savinkovtzi" were not only not supported by the population but were hated by them because they looted, murdered and burned—with very few exceptions.

These facts and others were a terrible blow to me.

The truth consists in the following: already in 1923 I reached the conclusion that it is impossible and perhaps unnecessary to struggle against the Bolsheviks. Impossible because we all (the Social-Revolutionaries, the Mensheviks, the Constitutional Democrats, the Savinkovtzi and the rest) are definitely beaten. Unnecessary—because if we all are beaten, then that means that the Russian people are not with us but with the Soviet Government. I did not speak to you about it. I did not speak about it to anybody, except to Mrs.

3. An agent-provocateur who helped Savinkov return to Russia.
4. Ditto.
5. Colonel S. E. Pavlovsky—Savinkov's most trusted man in Russia.

Derenthal and a little with my late mother who, as I remember, called me a "communist." I kept silent not because
I did not have the courage to acknowledge my defeat but
because, to acknowledge it, did not mean that I should
~~simply stand aside or go to the Riviera to live out my days~~
like a retired official; it meant for me the recognition of the
Soviet Government. And upon this I could not decide at
that time . . . and I continued up to the last to hold to my
former absolutely irreconcilable position, at least officially.
But I wrote *The Black Horse*. Did you read the last page
of it in its original version? Do you remember that I completely changed this page because unconsciously it gave the
impression that the novel was definitely in favour of the
Bolsheviks? I will tell you: if A.P. and E. had not come, I
would, probably in the autumn of 1923, talked to you and
not only to you alone, about my and our common mistake.
But there arrived "the friends from Moscow." You have not
forgotten, of course, what they told us: the émigrés have
lost their importance; they have no fighting material; the
old programmes are no use; a generation of "new" men has
grown up; these "new" men are carrying on the struggle
against the Bolshevik Government; they are fighting it having learned from it much which is foreign to us émigrés;
our duty, and especially mine, is to help this new generation.

"The friends from Moscow" opened new perspectives
before me. I did not believe much in these nor had I, personally, much faith in the "friends" (with the exception of
S.E.). You know that, but how could I speak about dis-
continuing the struggle if there was even a 20 percent chance
that they are not deceiving me? I began to think that my
pessimism was due to fatigue. And I decided to go to Russia.
What for? If an organisation really exists and not on foreign
money, not with the aid of our, the émigrés support, but
independently, drawing its forces from the peasants and the
workmen, then I must go and help this organisation, i.e.,
I must continue the struggle against the Bolsheviks with all

available means not excluding terror. But if the "friends from Moscow" deceived me, if there is nothing in Russia, then ... Draw your own conclusions. Not only did the "friends from Moscow" deceive me, but even the past (the Korotkevitchs[6] and the Pavlovskis[7] etc.) proved to be rotten.

There arose before me *the* question. It arose not in the Hotel Savoy but in the Lubianka on the eve of my trial. What shall I do? Shut myself up in silence and by this very silence continue to call for further struggle which in my eyes had already become useless, i.e., unrighteous, because the people are not with us but against us, or to have the courage to acknowledge my mistake and to recognise the Soviet Government?

I say "courage" because a fear came over me that I would be spattered with mud. Not by the émigrés, of course, but by my sister, by you, by Filossofov, i.e., the only persons who are near to me. It seems that so it has happened. ... But when I realised that in the eyes of millions of Russians I am not a liberator but an enemy of the people, when I understood that the workmen of Moscow will, without any compulsion, come and demand my death, which in their eyes I deserved, then my hesitation vanished. You know that the Court deliberated for four hours before passing sentence. Yes, this was "an amusing and silly farce." It is easy to die being conscious of one's righteousness but it is very hard to die when one feels that one is in the wrong. I wish that Filossofov may never have to go through such hours as I have gone through.

You will say, "It is not a question of the Moscow workmen and not even of the Russian people. It is a question of a struggle of two worlds. On the one side of the barricades

6. A leader of Savinkov's organization in Russia who was shot by the Bolsheviks.
7. Colonel E. Pavlovsky was Savinkov's most trusted man in Russia.

the old magnificent traditional European culture and on the
other side the 'advent of the Kham.'"[8]

No, Sidney, I have never fought for Europe and for
her doubtful magnificence. I am a Russian. I have been
fighting for Russia and for the Russian people. As regards
the advent of the "Kham," hear me out to the end.

It will soon be two months that I have been in prison.
Of course sitting in prison, one sees little, no matter how
indulgent the regulations may be. But nevertheless, I know
immeasurably more about the situation in Russia than I knew
while abroad. With what are the émigrés fed? By the articles
of Miliukoff, Chernoff, Douskova, in the best cases by
Prokopovitch and Braikevevitch and in the very best case
by the reports of our agents and of the agents of some foreign
contre-espionage organisation.

But all these "writers" write nonsense, not excluding
even Braikevevitch because they write of imaginings conceived in their dreams. And the "agents" report what pleases
their chiefs. And the fog grows. In this fog we wander about
like the blind, repeating always the same worn out phrases.
We pusillanimously persuade ourselves and others that the
Bolsheviks must unavoidably fall. The day before yesterday
we were building our hopes on Denikin, yesterday upon the
"Greens," today upon an economic and financial crash. Our
hopes burst like soap bubbles but we continue to beguile
ourselves like children. How many fairytales I have buried
here in the Lubianka.

I will begin with a little thing; with the G.P.U. What
are the Chekists? Criminals and born executioners? Derenthal, when he was arrested seriously asked: "Are we going
to be tortured?" Well, then, I will tell you. I have met men
in the G.P.U. to whom I am used since my boyhood and

8. This can best be translated as "the advent of the 'Under-Man,'
    the anti-social savage, incapable of culture whom the Revo-
    lution has brought to the surface."

who are spiritually nearer to me than the mutterers of the
"National Centre"[9] or of the Foreign Delegation of the "So-
cialist-Revolutionary party." I have met convinced Revolutionaries. They are executing? Yes! But have not we also
been executing? Take for instance the trial of Gnilorybov.[10]
I read his case from A to Z. He was shot only after he had
been shown to be an informer, after he had falsely testified
against a number of innocent people, had broken the head
of the investigating Magistrate with a bottle and had attempted to escape, having tied up his guard in the bathroom.

Take now the "martyred" Social-Revolutionaries! For
preparing terroristic acts they were sentenced only to 5 years
imprisonment, which according to the laws here means only
two and a half years, and they were not clapped into prison
but were interned in the country in one of the Soviet estates.

And what of the prisons here? Nobody is kept in prison
here for more than three years and even then one is given
periodical leave to have a day in town. In which other
country would that be possible? But as I have already said:
this is merely a trivial matter. It is not a question of the
G.P.U. or of the prisons. It is not even a question whether
the Bolsheviks have received from the Germans 70 million
Marks. (No, they have not received them . . . Bourtzeff is
wrong about it.) The main question of course is: Is Russia
recovering? That the people are for the Soviet Government
there is no doubt whatsoever. Without the support of the
popular masses, would it have been possible to vanquish
the Whites, to annihilate the Greens, to overcome the Volga
famine, to survive the murderous blockade and the unsuccessful war with Poland? Think, my dear friend, about this,
forgetting for a moment the diary of Madame Gippius[11]

9. Patriotic non-party Russian organization in Paris.
10. One of former supporters who went over to the Bolsheviks.
11. Famous Russian poet and writer, wife of D. S. Merezhkovski,
    the writer and philosopher.

about the "sufferings" of the intelligentsia. Yes, there was a time when everybody, including the intelligentsia, had to feed only on dried-fish soup. But in order not to surrender on such nourishment, but to beat down the attacks of Denikin and of Koltchak and Yudenitch and finally of Wrangel, an enormous enthusiasm was required not only in individuals not only in Chekists and in the Red Army but in the entire mass of the people.

Think of the "Marie-Louises" during the Campagne de France in 1814. Just think if the French had been offered the above menu during the last war! How long would Paris have held? The Bolsheviks have withstood the struggle for existence, for the right to live on this earth and they have been victorious in this struggle. Of course this is not all. Another problem is waiting, the problem of the reconstruction of Russia. Has the Soviet Government been tackling this problem?

In Moscow there are shops, theatres, cinemas, motor-cars, tramways, electric light, cabs and even fast trotting horses. This is, of course, no proof. The proof is only in statistical data. Take Zinoviev's report to the 13th Congress. You have not read it, naturally. But I assert that if in his words only one quarter is the truth, then it is perfectly clear that the revolutionary chaos is finished and that, albeit slowly, the economic situation of Russia is being resuscitated and that, not despite of but *with* the help of the Soviet Government and the Russian Communist Party. You, abroad are still dreaming of 1918–1919; you still see the dried-fish soup, the darkness, the looting, the executions, the typhus, and the lice. All this does not exist anymore. In Russia there is order. The fields are sown and the sowing is increasing with every year. Industrial production is rising. The Tchervonetz is higher than the Pound Sterling. You do not believe all this? You think that dust is being thrown into my eyes? No, I tell you again: The crisis is past. It is already proved that it is possible for a country to recover without landlords and without the big bourgeoisie. But you are still awaiting

for Soviet Russia to go bust because England does not give
her any money; England has not given any money but the
budget has been balanced without a deficit. A new state is
emerging different from a European one. I say "emerging";
I do not say "has emerged." Of course there is still a long
road to travel; there is immense work and great troubles and
privations lie in front of us. But we Russians are tens of
millions. And these tens of millions want to live a human
life and under all circumstances *with* the Soviet Government, i.e., with its very own Government. Remember this!
Some day, very soon, you will convince yourself that not
you are right but I am.

Russia is recovering but abroad they say that she is
finally perishing and that the Russian people await a "Mes-
siah." According to émigré information, the working men
are starving. Braikevevitch wrote that the Bolsheviks are
exploiting the working man. This, of course, is nonsense,
just as it is nonsense that the Bolsheviks are exploiting the
N.E.P.[12] The N.E.P. is being combated by the Cooperatives,
and to Siberia are sent not merchants but profiteers, i.e.,
sharks, who ought to be exiled.

The Red Army? The Command is Red of course but
the rank and file? Where, in what country is the soldier so
cared for as here?

There remain the peasants! Very well. I have before
me a book called *The Old and the New Life*, an ethnograph-
ical investigation of the Archangel and Tcherepovetz Prov-
inces, which were proverbially among the most backward.
When I read that the Samoyed, returning home, carries with
him a book on aviation or that in the Kola Peninsula library
huts are being opened and that beyond the Arctic Circle, in
a fishing village, debates are being held upon the question
whether God exists or not and that little children are singing

12. The "New Economic Policy," instituted in 1921 but virtually
    abolished by 1924. Also applied to all those who profited
    from this policy.

a song: "Oh, my God why do you laze about, why do you lie about with the Virgin instead of working," then I cannot help saying that the depths of peasant life have been shaken to their foundations and that Russia has been reborn completely.

By the way, about religion and the religious movements, the churches are full, but with old men and old women. Few men are to be seen. In the country there are now four religions: The Greek Orthodox (no difference is made between the Tikhon Church and the Living Church); "Wizardry," which has appeared in great strength because Paganism and Witchcraft are, like all other faiths, not prosecuted, the Baptist Religion and the Atheist Religion. (Nearly the whole of the young generation belongs to the Atheist Religion.) You may not like this but it is an undeniable fact, just as it is a fact that there are now over six hundred thousand Communists, about one million members of the League of Communist Youth and over three hundred thousand Communist boy scouts, i.e., a total of about two million adults, youths, and children in the Russian Communist Party.

It is necessary to state the truth: the Soviet Government is winning over the villages. It is winning them because it is sincerely and honestly aiming to ameliorate the condition of the peasants. Could the Mensheviks or Social-Revolutionaries have done it? Avksintiev and Dan, for instance? The Monarchists of course are not worth mentioning.

I shall return to my personal position. That miserable Vishniak (have you heard about him?) has written that my "speciality" is to betray everybody . . . Whom have I betrayed? An idea? But the "White" and the "Green" ideas have long ago ceased to exist; it is not I who have compromised them. The non-existing organisation of A.P. and E.? Filossofov, Artzybashov Portugalov?[13] But these do not

13. Co-editors of *For Freedom* and former intimate friends of Savinkov.

fight the Bolsheviks; in reality they just "live" and besides, there is nothing against their returning to Russia. They are offended at my offer of repatriation. Let them, they will accept sooner or later; they will be compelled to accept it or to remain émigrés forever. The Social-Revolutionaries? But the Social-Revolutionaries have unjustly excluded me from the party to which I belonged for fourteen years; in 1918 they published my description in the press in the hope that the Bolsheviks would arrest me; they surrounded me with spies in Kazan; they gave me the most dangerous tasks to do—again, in the hope that I would not return from them; they libelled and slandered the Constitutional Democrats. But they acted exactly like the Social-Revolutionaries. Do you remember the systematic lies of Miliukov; that I gave my consent to the destruction of the Russian Churches by the Poles, that diamonds had been stolen from me, that I am a Markov II?[14] ... No, it is a long time since any ties existed between me and the S.R.'s or the C.D.'s. How dare they, then, say that I betrayed them? Who else remains? The Monarchists? But they have consciously and deliberately betrayed members of our League to the Bolsheviks and about me they have spoken only in favour of my execution.

I, a Russian, betrayed the foreigners? Have I ever doubted that they are prepared to help me only in as much as they think that I can be useful to them? You know that I love France almost as much as you love Russia. But did not Noulens deceive me before the Yaroslav rising? It is time to speak out loud and to say that the foreigners have only pursued their own interests and that we have nothing to thank them for! I am happy that I am now independent and I am happy that I am no longer an émigré.

That, my dear friend, is what I wanted to tell you. I do not think that I will have convinced you; nor did I have this object in view: I only wanted you to know what has hap-

14. Notorious Russian Revolutionary.

pened to me in Moscow and also that you should know that
Russia is not what it seems from London or Paris. I conclude
with what I have always told you: I shall remember you
and love you always even if you will deny me and throw
mud at me, even then shall I not deny you.

My humble regards to your wife.

My address: c/o Citizen V. V. Malinovsky

> First Mieshtchanskaya Street, No. 43,
> lodging No. 1

You need not add anything more; it will be forwarded to
me.

> I embrace you,

> Yours

> signed   (B. Savinkov)

P.S. You may do what you like with this letter, i.e., if you
find it necessary, you may publish it, in extracts or in full.

Appendix III

Notes on a recorded interview with General Alexander Orlov made by the office of the Senate Internal Security Subcommittee on February 11, 1955. (The closed session hearings of Orlov's testimony to the Subcommittee began on September 28, 1955.)

ALEXANDER ORLOV

Notes on Interview with Orlov on February 11, 1955.

SPANISH GOLD

Orlov was placed in charge of Soviet intelligence in the Spanish civil war. In about October 1936, he received a highly secret coded telegram emanating from Stalin which directed him to take charge of the shipment of the entire gold reserve of the Spanish Loyalist government to the USSR. The Spanish Loyalists acceded to this request because they feared that the gold reserve would fall into the hands of Franco. Orlov made detailed arrangements with Foreign Minister Negrin and Treasury Chief Aspe. Twenty trucks were assigned to transport the gold from certain caves near Cartagena to the docks where four Soviet ships were waiting. Each box weighed 145 pounds. The Spanish Loyalists got no receipt for the gold. They were told they would get such a receipt from Moscow. The shipment was assigned fictitiously to Blackstone of the Bank of America. Russian sailors and tankists were assigned to the loading of the gold. There were in all 156 carloads. Incidentally, Orlov noticed a discrepancy between his figures and those of Treasury Chief Aspe.

The consignment was sent to Odessa, Russia. Orlov notified Yezhov, head of the NKVD, that all was ready. Arrangements were made for protection of the ships by the Spanish fleet and the Russian fleet.

At a banquet in Moscow after the arrival of the gold, Stalin is alleged to have said, "They have as little chance of seeing their gold again as of seeing their ears." The value of the gold shipment was about £1,150,000. Aspe was aghast when Orlov gave him no receipt for the gold, so Orlov offered that certain Spanish bank cashiers accompany the shipment to Moscow, which they did. He doubts that they ever had any chance to check on the gold. They were kept in Moscow for three or four years and then went to Mexico.

Orlov made the suggestion that some efforts should be made to encourage defectors who are tied up with the Malenkov regime. He believed that if we held out an offer of immunity, we might get some important defectors.

INTERNATIONAL REFUGEE APPARATUS

Mr. Orlov is in a position to testify about the ramified apparatus used by Moscow to transport and take care of its operatives in various countries when they have to flee from place to place.

INTELLIGENCE SCHOOLS

Mr. Orlov is in a position to testify as to the nature of intelligence schools he helped to establish for picked personnel. Confidentially, he mentioned the name of Alexander Korokov, now the head of the Soviet underground intelligence apparatus who was formerly an elevator boy in his building and whom Orlov helped to train. Orlov also knew Tagliatti, head of the Italian Communist Party. Orlov once saved his life. Orlov thinks that Tagliatti hates the Moscow regime and, if properly and secretly approached, could possibly be bargained with.

SPANISH

Orlov knew of the activities of Codovilla, also known as Medina, head of the Communist Party of Argentina, who was active in Spain.

Orlov also met Robert Minor of the American Communist Party in Spain, and comments on his complete servility to him and other Moscow representatives.

Orlov organized intelligence training schools in Spain for both British and American operatives who thereafter received certain special privileges.

ANDRÉ MARTY

Orlov thinks that, if properly and secretly approached, André Marty, French Communist leader who has recently been deposed, could be persuaded to write his memoirs, disclosing the inside workings of the French Communist Party.

Appendix IV

Letter written by General Orlov to Robert Morris (now Judge Morris), Chief Counsel to the Senate Internal Security Subcommittee, dated April 23, 1956. In Life *magazine of the same date, Orlov revealed that Stalin had been an assiduous officer of the Okhrana, the Tsarist secret police. Stalin was obsessed with fear that this would one day be exposed—hence one of the main reasons for his "elimination" of any and all who might conceivably learn of his guilty secret.*

Mr. Robert Morris   April 23, 1956
Chief Counsel
Internal Security Subcommittee
United States Senate

Dear Mr. Morris,

     I hope that you have read my book <u>The Secret History of Stalin's Crimes</u>, a copy of which I left with you when I had the pleasure of meeting you for the first time at Point Pleasant. On page 240 of that book, in the chapter about the execution of the Red Army generals, I alluded to "one of Stalin's most horrible secrets which, when disclosed, will throw light on many things that seemed so incomprehensible in Stalin's behavior."

     This week I revealed that secret in my article published in Life Magazine under the title "WHAT KHRUSHCHEV ISN'T TELLING: STALIN'S GUILTIEST SECRET." Beside revealing one of the most guarded secrets of the Kremlin, this article explains the sudden turnabout of Russia's present masters in denouncing and downgrading Stalin. I hope that some day the Kremlin leaders will confirm the truthfulness of my article in the same way as Khrushchev has recently confirmed the authenticity of the account of Stalin's frame-ups given by me in my book. I shall be pleased if you read my article which is in the current issue of Life.

     I have been following with great interest your investigation of the circumstances which led to the return of the five Soviet sailors to Russia.

     I am going to be in Washington soon and I hope to see you then.

     With kindest regards from my wife and myself,

Alexander Orlov

Appendix V

The Reports of the Hearings of the U.S. Senate Committee of the Judiciary's Subcommittee on Internal Security constitute a unique and probably the greatest source available to the free world on Communist penetration and subversion. One of the Subcommittee's longest investigations ever undertaken was that into the Institute of Pacific Relations (I.P.R.). Intelligence circles have described the investigation into I.P.R. as "comprehensive, meticulous, and masterly." A few miscellaneous pages to indicate the depth of the investigation are appended.

INSTITUTE OF PACIFIC RELATIONS

HEARINGS

BEFORE THE

SUBCOMMITTEE TO INVESTIGATE THE ADMINISTRATION
OF THE INTERNAL SECURITY ACT AND OTHER
INTERNAL SECURITY LAWS

OF THE

COMMITTEE ON THE JUDICIARY
UNITED STATES SENATE

EIGHTY-SECOND CONGRESS

FIRST SESSION

ON

THE INSTITUTE OF PACIFIC RELATIONS

PART 2

AUGUST 9, 14, 16, 20, 22, AND 23, 1951

Printed for the use of the Committee on the Judiciary

UNITED STATES
GOVERNMENT PRINTING OFFICE
WASHINGTON : 1951

2248

Budenz, presently assistant professor at Fordham University, and former member of the American Communist Politburo, said he had heard IPR described in a Politburo meeting as "the Little Red Schoolhouse for teaching certain people in Washington how to think with the Soviet Union in the Far East" (p. 517).

Maj. Gen. Charles A. Willoughby, chief of intelligence for the Far East and United Nations Command, declared "the conclusion could be arrived at" that the Japanese branch of IPR was "used as a spy ring for Russian Communists and the Russian Red Army" (p. 364). Alexander Barmine, chief of the Russian unit in the State Department's Voice of America and former brigadier general of the Red Army, said he had been told by Soviet intelligence officers that IPR was "a cover shop for military intelligence work in the Pacific area" (p. 202). Igor Bogolepov, another refugee from Red tyranny who was once counselor of the Soviet Foreign Office, gave the following testimony:

* * * As one of my former comrades expressed it, it (the IPR) is like a double-way track. On one line you get information from America through this institute. On the other hand, you send information which you would like to implant in American brains through the same channel of the institute. * * *

Mr. MORRIS. When you talk about two-way track, do you mean that military intelligence was extracted from outside the Soviet Union through the medium of the Institute of Pacific Relations?

Mr. BOGOLEPOV. That is right.

Mr. MORRIS. And on the other hand, by the out-way track you mean information that you wanted to impart to the outside world was transmitted through that medium?

Mr. BOGOLEPOV. Yes (p. 4491).

Senator EASTLAND. Propaganda, you mean. Soviet propaganda that the Foreign Office desired implanted in foreign minds would be sent through the facilities of the Institute of Pacific Relations. That is what you mean?

Mr. BOGOLEPOV. That is mostly propaganda, but I would say even a little more than propaganda, because not only organizational propaganda but even the organization of a network of fellow travelers in your and other countries (p. 4492).

*   *   *   *   *   *   *

Mr. MORRIS. Did you know that the Soviet organization used the Institute of Pacific Relations to collect information not only in the United States but on other countries, such as Japan and China?

Mr. BOGOLEPOV. It was my impression that, at that time—I mean before the war—when I was in the Soviet Union, the Soviet intelligence was more interested not in the United States of America, but in Japan and other countries which were in direct conflict with the Soviet Union. It was also my impression that the Institute of Pacific Relations was merely used by Soviet intelligence in order to get, via America, the information on Japan and China and Great Britain (p. 4590).

Which of these descriptions of the Institute of Pacific Relations are the true ones?

This was the fundamental question to which the subcommittee addressed itself. In seeking the answer, it weighed the testimony of 66 witnesses, and studied the contents of approximately 20,000 documents, including letters, memoranda, pamphlets, magazine articles, and books.

STATEMENT BY THE CHAIRMAN

The subcommittee's open hearings began July 25, 1951, with the following statement by the chairman:

One of the lines of inquiry undertaken by the Internal Security Subcommittee concerned the extent to which subversive forces may have influenced or sought to influence the formulation and execution of our foreign policy.

FIELD, FREDERICK V.—Continued
Subject of action by agency of American Government or a foreign non-Communist government on grounds involving loyalty or national security.
Affiliated with: Amerasia (p. 35); American Friends of the Chinese People, official organ: China Today, (p. 116); Federated Press (p. 4152); Friends of Chinese Democracy (p. 622); Russian War Relief (p. 295); Soviet Russia Today (p. 102); Committee for a Democratic Far Eastern Policy (p. 4610–11).
Signer of a statement attacking the United States for "suppressing the Chinese masses and fomenting civil wars among them."

FRIEDMAN, IRVING F., research associate (exhibit 801):
Affiliated with: Amerasia (exhibit 1355).

FRIEDMAN, JULIAN R., participant in conferences (p. 710); writer (p. 711).
Identified as a member of the Communist Party by one or more duly sworn witnesses. Denied.
Affiliated with: China Aid Council (p. 1513); Committee for a Democratic Far Eastern Policy (p. 771).

GERLACH, TALITHA, supporter (exhibit 1334):
Identified as a member of the Communist Party by one or more duly sworn witnesses.
Out of the country or otherwise unavailable for subpena.
Affiliated with: American Committee in Aid of Chinese Industrial Cooperatives, also known as Indusco, Inc. (p. 3793); China Aid Council (p. 1513); Committee for a Democratic Far Eastern Policy (p. 2789); Friends of Chinese Democracy (p. 622).

GOSHAL, KUMAR, writer (exhibit 1334):
Identified as a member of the Communist Party by one or more duly sworn witnesses.
Affiliated with: Amerasia (exhibit 1355); Committee for a Democratic Far Eastern Policy (p. 2789).

GRAVES, MORTIMER, trustee (p. 713):
Affiliated with: Amerasia (exhibit 1355); American Russian Institute (p. 4091).
Signer of a statement defending the Soviet Union as "a consistent bulwark against war and aggression."

GREENBERG, MICHAEL, managing editor, Pacific Affairs (exhibit 801):
Collaborated with agents of the Soviet intelligence apparatus as shown by sworn testimony.
Subject of action by agency of American Government or a foreign non-Communist government on grounds involving loyalty or national security.
Out of the country or otherwise unavailable for subpena.
Affiliated with: Amerasia (exhibit 1355); American Committee in Aid of Chinese Industrial Cooperatives, also known as Indusco, Inc. (p. 3794).

HISS, ALGER, trustee (p. 134):
Identified as a member of the Communist Party by one or more duly sworn witnesses.
Collaborated with agents of the Soviet Intelligence apparatus as shown by sworn testimony.
Subject of action by agency of American government or a foreign non-Communist government on grounds involving loyalty or national security.

HOLLAND, WILLIAM L., research secretary; secretary-general; editor, Pacific Affairs; executive vice-chairman (exhibit 801):
Affiliated with: Amerasia (exhibit 1355); China Aid Council (p. 1513).

HSU, YUNG YING, research associate (exhibit 801):
Made one or more trips to Communist territory.
Affiliated with: Amerasia (exhibit 1355).

JAFFE, PHILIP R. (James W. Philips), conference participant (exhibit 1334); financial contributor (p. 71; exhibit 1383):
Identified as a member of the Communist Party by one or more sworn witnesses.
Made one or more trips to Communist territory.
Writer for official publications of the Communist Party or the Communist International or for a Communist government or pro-Communist press services.
Subject of action by agency of American Government or a foreign non-Communist government on grounds involving loyalty or national security.
Affiliated with: Amerasia (p. 35); Amerian Committee in Aid of Chinese Industrial Cooperatives, also known as Indusco, Inc. (p. 3794); American

Appendices

A. Stewart, Maxwell S. Stewart, Anna Louise Strong, Mary Van Kleeck, Ella Winter, Victor A. Yakhontoff, and others.

No claim is made here that the persons responsible for this marked devotion to Soviet interests were actually paid to do such work, although it is true that Miss Strong was actually employed by the Moscow Daily News. It is more conceivable that these individuals were motivated primarily by their complete acceptance of the Soviet philosophy to the point of subordinating themselves voluntarily to its will. As Bogolepov described the Soviet practice, "We do not pay the agents. The agents work out of their sympathy toward the Soviet Union" (p. 4497).

IPR AND SOVIET INTELLIGENCE

It will be remembered that Bogolepov and Barmine both referred to the IPR as a cover organization for Soviet military intelligence. Our subcommittee cannot claim sufficient access to the innermost depths of the world-wide Communist network in all its deviousness to be able to supply the full picture. We can only sketch the pattern as it unfolds from the witnesses and documents available to us as a Senate subcommittee.

This report already has indicated the number of officers and members of the board of the Soviet IPR who have been cited by witnesses as directly associated with Soviet military intelligence including A. S. Svanidze, G. N. Voitinski, Abramson, Mekhonoshin, Avorin, and Kara-Murza. Also previously mentioned have been those who have been listed among American IPR personnel as collaborating with agents of the Soviet intelligence apparatus including: Solomon Adler, Joseph F. Barnes, Frank V. Coe, Henry Collins, Lauchlin Currie, Laurence Duggan, Israel Epstein, John K. Fairbank, Frederick V. Field, Michael Greenberg, Alger Hiss, Owen Lattimore, Duncan C. Lee, Robert T. Miller, Hozumi Ozaki, Fred Poland, Lee Pressman, Kimikazu Saionji, Agnes Smedley, Guenther Stein, Anna Louise Strong, Harry Dexter White, and Victor A. Yakhontoff, plus those involved in the Amerasia case, namely John Stewart Service, Andrew Roth, Kate Mitchell, and Philip Jaffe. We propose to amplify this picture from the record.

When Lattimore was before the subcommittee, he was asked whether he assumed that the Soviet officials he had dealt with in Moscow were intelligence agents. He replied:

I assume they were all connected with the Soviet Government in one form or another. * * * Of course, at the present time, I would generally assume that any Soviet citizen or subject is an intelligence agent or a potential one (p. 3325).

Nevertheless, he found nothing irregular in his having asked at the Soviet IPR conference on April 6, 1936, whether "there was any special interest in the U.S.S.R. about the question of air bases in the Pacific" (p. 3323).

Although the work of V. E. Motylev, president of the Soviet IPR, presented as simply that of a geographer in charge of the Great Soviet World Atlas, Professor Poppe has advanced a somewhat different version. "Mapping and publication of maps" he declared, "is controlled by the NKVD (Soviet secret police). The only agency publishing maps and permitted to do so is the chief geographic and geodetic department of the NKVD" (p. 2697).

Edward C. Carter made sustained efforts to aid him in this project, so that as Carter put it, "his unusual gifts could be utilized during the war emergency" (p. 25). One letter dated February 18, 1942, written by Field, indicated that he understood that Lattimore had taken up the matter of the commission with Currie (p. 19), a fact which Field acknowledged while on the witness stand (p. 108).

Currie was responsible for setting up a conference in Washington, on October 12, 1942, between himself, Sumner Welles, then Under Secretary of State, and Earl Browder and Robert Minor, then officials of the Communist Party (p. 598 ff.). This conference terminated with Welles handing to Browder a memorandum declaring that the United States desired unity between the Chinese Government and the Communist forces in China; that the State Department felt that civil strife in China was at all times unfortunate; that both the armies of the Nationalist government and the Communist armies were fighting the Japanese; that the State Department viewed with skepticism alarmist accounts of the menace of communism in China (p. 599).

This memorandum was printed in full in the Daily Worker of October 16, 1942, and was used extensively by the Communists all over the world to give prestige to the Chinese Communists.[8]

The subcommittee found records in the files of the Institute of Pacific Relations which showed that Currie used White House stationary in giving endorsements to the institute (exhibit 1229, p. 8).

On November 9, 1942, Michael Greenberg[9] was appointed to a position with the Board of Economic Warfare and was assigned to and shared an office with Lauchlin Currie in the White House. Greenberg made use of White House stationery in his correspondence (pp. 413–414).

Greenberg had succeeded Owen Lattimore in 1941 as the managing editor of Pacific Affairs.[10]

Elizabeth Bentley testified he was a Communist in the IPR cell when she recruited him for espionage work in Washington (p. 413). Prof. Karl Wittfogel testified that he told the security officers of Greenberg's Communist persuasions and was surprised that he turned up in the White House (p. 281). Prof. George Taylor, of the University of Washington, testified that Greenberg was so blatant in his beliefs that he (Taylor) was shocked when Greenberg obtained a White House position.[10a] As Taylor put it, a blind man would have perceived that he (Greenberg) was following the Communist Party line (p. 345).

Another influential IPR person who used the White House for a mailing address was John K. Fairbank (pp. 427, 3805). Fairbank explained he did this because Lauchlin Currie was assistant to the President in charge of far-eastern matters and was a focal person for

[8] Several years later it was shown that John S. Service mentioned this and asked that more such letters be issued by the U. S. Government (p. 826).
[9] Greenberg was a British Communist who had emigrated to the United States and became interested in the IPR (p. 281).
[10] Even though he bore the title managing editor, the IPR correspondence and the testimony revealed that Greenberg was the actual editor of Pacific Affairs and that he was running it "in the Lattimore tradition." Several controversies arose in Pacific Affairs which indicated that Greenberg was steering the publication along the Communist line (pp. 416–417).
[10a] Taylor testified that Currie was friendly and invited him to his office every Wednesday until he, Taylor, wrote a memorandum saying that the hope of Kuomintang-Communist cooperation was negligible and that the United States should provide arms to Chiang Kai-shek to shoot the Communists. After that not only was he never invited to come back, but he never again saw Currie (p. 348).

Senator FERGUSON. Did Greenberg ever deliver any papers to you?

Mr. BENTLEY. Yes; he delivered information via Mildred Price to me. He was extremely temperamental and I thought it unwise to have h..n meet me.

Senator FERGUSON. Did this information come out of the White House?

Miss BENTLEY. Yes; it was mostly on the Far East, on China.

Senator FERGUSON. It came out of the White House and he was assistant to Lauchlin Currie?

Miss BENTLEY. Yes; or one of the assistants. I don't know whether he was the only one.

Mr. MORRIS. The nature of the exhibits is they showed that Greenberg succeeded Owen Lattimore as editor for the Institute of Pacific Relations.

The CHAIRMAN. You are referring to what exhibits?

Mr. MORRIS. Exhibits 8, 7, and 51.

The CHAIRMAN. Very well. All I want you to do is to identify the exhibits and their connection with the party named.

Mr. MORRIS. We will have to get that, Senator. I would like to comment upon exhibit No. 67, which was taken from the institute files. It is from Michael Greenberg on the letterhead of the White House in Washington, addressed to Miss Hilda Austern, Institute of Pacific Relations, 129 East Fifty-second Street, New York, N. Y.

DEAR HILDA: Mr. Currie has asked me to write you about the sending of IPR publications to William D. Carter in New Delhi, India. He says that he is baffled by the problem.

The only thing I can suggest is that you select a few books and try to get them out via OWI.

Sincerely yours,

MICHAEL.

That was introduced as exhibit 67 at the open hearings of August 7, 1951.

I would like to introduce, Mr. Chairman, at this time a letter dated May 23, 1943, from Mr. Y. Y. Hsu to Mr. Carter. I will ask Mr. Mandel if he will verify that that was taken from the institute files.

Mr. MANDEL. This letter was taken from the files of the Institute of Pacific Relations and is dated May 23, 1942, addressed to "Dear Mr. Carter," and it is from Yung-ying Hsu.

Enclosed please find a memorandum which Miss Mildred Price worked out with my assistance. She has submitted a copy to Mr. Mills of the CIO Greater New York Industrial Council. The memo is written, by the way, on Mr. Mills' specific request. Miss Price would like to have a conference with you to discuss the same problem. She also suggests my participation. The present memorandum is based upon findings in my two previous memos which have been submitted to you and Mr. Holland. There are a few new points which I intended to examine more closely as a part of my research work. These have been included in the present document in the form of general statements. I believe they are reasonably correct. I have not been able to secure an additional copy of the present memo for Mr. Holland. I am sure you will make the enclosed copy available to him as you see fit.

Mr. MORRIS. Mr. Chairman, I would like to introduce that into evidence as the next consecutive exhibit.

The CHAIRMAN. It may be inserted and properly identified.

(The document referred to was marked "Exhibit No. 101" and is as follows:)

Mr. Morris. Mr. Budenz, two previous witnesses have identified Michael Greenberg as a member of the Communist Party. Did you know that Michael Greenberg is a member of the Communist Party?

Mr. Budenz. I knew him from official communications to be a member of the Communist Party, yes, sir.

Mr. Morris. Mr. Chairman, we have already shown Mr. Greenberg is connected with the Institute of Pacific Relations, but I think we have one inquiry by Senator Ferguson which has not been answered.

Mr. Mandel. Senator Ferguson asked about the naturalization of Michael Greenberg. Our files show that Michael Greenberg was naturalized in the United States District Court of Washington, D. C., June 6, 1944, certificate No. 6270908.

Senator Smith. Where was he from?

Mr. Mandel. England.

Mr. Morris. May the record so show?

Mr. Budenz, do you know Andrew Roth to be a member of the Communist Party?

Mr. Budenz. Yes, sir, from official communications. My impression is that I met Andrew Roth but I am not sure. He was very active, particularly during the Amerasia difficulties in sending suggestions to the Communist leaders.

Mr. Morris. Do you know his book, Dilemma in Japan?

Mr. Budenz. Yes, sir. This book, Dilemma in Japan, was submitted to the Politburo for reading before it was published.

Mr. Morris. You know that from your own knowledge?

Mr. Budenz. Yes, sir; I saw at least what purported to be a copy of it. It was to be given to several people and I didn't read it.

Mr. Morris. Who published Dilemma in Japan?

Mr. Budenz. I think it is Little, Brown & Co.

Mr. Morris. It so states in that article?

Mr. Budenz. That was my remembrance.

Mr. Morris. Could you comment any further on Dilemma in Japan as used by the Communist Party, Mr. Budenz?

Mr. Budenz. Well, this particular photostat that has been given me, which is the Daily Worker of September 12, 1945—the date is obscure, but it's 1945—page 8, Seeds of New Pearl Harbor still in Japan, Writer Warns, by Samuel Sillen, was a leading article in order to focus attention on Japan, which the Communist leaders were on orders to advance everywhere they could. In this book, Lieutenant Roth attacks very sharply Under Secretary of State Grew, or rather former Under Secretary of State Grew, because Grew had resigned while this book was in the course of being prepared or published rather.

Mr. Morris. Mr. Chairman, I would like this photostat, if it is authenticated by Mr. Mandel, to be introduced into the record and marked as the next consecutive exhibit.

Mr. Mandel. This is a photostat of the Daily Worker of September 12, 1945, page 8, which was reproduced at my direction.

Senator Smith. So ordered.

Dr. Wittfogel. Exactly.

Mr. Morris. Who was that contact?

Dr. Wittfogel. This was Mr. Julian Gumperz, who at that time lived in New York.

Mr. Morris. Dr. Wittfogel, will you relate the circumstances of your visit with Mr. Carter at that time?

Dr. Wittfogel. I came to see him. Mr. Carter was there with two or three lady secretaries. After I had introduced myself, Mr. Carter asked me a question which embarrassed me no end, or more puzzled me than embarrassed me.

This was his first question: "Dr. Wittfogel, are you a member of the German Communist Party?"

I was not quite accustomed to this kind of thing, and I thought maybe in America everything is different from anywhere else.

I found out later in regard to this question, it was not frequently repeated here.   It was a more individual thing.

I answered, "I was, but I am not now," whereupon Mr. Carter smiled somewhat and said, "Well, in any case, you are not a member of the Chinese Communist Party."

Mr. Morris. Dr. Wittfogel, did he have the impression that you were still friendly with the German Communist Party?

Dr. Wittfogel. We did not go further into this.

Mr. Sourwine. Mr. Morris, Dr. Wittfogel has already testified at that time and subsequent to that time he had done nothing overtly which would give anyone any notice he had broken with the Communist Party.

Mr. Morris. Is that so?

Dr. Wittfogel. Yes.

Mr. Morris. So, at that time, when you told Mr. Carter that you had been a member of the German Communist Party, he had reason to believe that was the atmosphere in which you were presently discussing the Institute of Pacific Relations?

Dr. Wittfogel. I do not know what was in his mind. It is a sheer guess, I would say, and that smile unfortunately no television has preserved for eternity.

I had the feeling he didn't believe me, even the fact I technically was no longer a member of the party. I did not discuss it with him.

Mr. Morris. His only reply was, "At least you are not a member of the Chinese Communist Party"?

Dr. Wittfogel. That is right.

Mr. Morris. While you were in England, did you ever meet Michael Greenberg?

Dr. Wittfogel. I was in Cambridge.   I met him there.

Mr. Morris. Will you tell us the circumstances?

Dr. Wittfogel. I saw him there among English Communist friends and he was, according to the general attitude toward him and his own behavior, an organized Communist.

Mr. Morris. You met Michael Greenberg at that time as a Communist?

Dr. Wittfogel. I hadn't seen his card, but I had seen him under circumstances which would indicate as clearly as you can in this way that this was his position.

INSTITUTE OF PACIFIC RELATIONS

Mr. Morris. Will you tell us what position Michael Greenberg held in the Institute?

Mr. Mandel. Senator Pat McCarran wrote to the Department of State inquiring as to the position of Michael Greenberg. On July 16, 1951, a reply was received from the Department of State from Mr. Carlisle H. Humelsine, Deputy Under Secretary, and I quote from that letter:

Michael Greenberg is not now an employee of the Department. He entered the Department on September 27, 1945, by transfer from the Foreign Economic Administration, under the provisions of Executive Order 9630. He was separated from the Department by reduction in force on June 15, 1946.

Another letter on the same matter came from the United States Civil Service Commission dated July 13, 1951, and signed by Robert Ramspeck, chairman, and states:

Michael Greenberg was appointed to a position with the Board of Economic Warfare on November 9, 1942. On July 7, 1944, he was transferred to the Foreign Economic Administration and on September 27, 1945, he was transferred to the Department of State. His employment was terminated due to reduction in force on June 15, 1946. In connection with his employment with the Foreign Economic Administration, an investigation of Mr. Greenberg was conducted by the Civil Service Commission to determine his general qualifications for Federal employment. As a result of this investigation Mr. Greenberg was barred from competing in civil-service examinations on March 7, 1947, because of questionable loyalty.

The Chairman. Do you want those inserted?

Mr. Morris. Yes, and marked with the next exhibit number.

The Chairman. It may be inserted.

(The document referred to was marked "Exhibit No. 68" and is as follows:)

Exhibit No. 68

Michael Greenberg

To: Hon. Senator McCarran.
From: Robert Ramspeck, chairman.

Michael Greenberg was appointed to a position with the Board of Economic Warfare on November 9, 1942. On July 7, 1944, he was transferred to the Foreign Economic Administration and on September 27, 1945, he was transferred to the Department of State. His employment was terminated due to reduction in force on June 15, 1946. In connection with his employment with the Foreign Economic Administration an investigation of Mr. Greenberg was conducted by the Civil Service Commission to determine his general qualifications for Federal employment. As a result of this investigation, Mr. Greenberg was barred from competing in civil-service examinations on March 7, 1947, because of questionable loyalty.

Information received from: United States Civil Service Commission, Washington, D. C., July 13, 1951.

To: Hon. Senator McCarran.
From: Mr. Carlisle H. Humelsine, Deputy Under Secretary.

Michael Greenberg is not now an employee of the Department. He entered the Department on September 27, 1945, by transfer from the Foreign Economic Administration under the provisions of Executive Order 9630. He was separated from the Department by reduction in force on June 15, 1946.

Information received from: Department of State, July 16, 1951.

Talitha Gerlach was reported out of the country, as was Michael Greenberg, for whom the last address we have is Trinity College, Cambridge, England, and we also heard from Mr. Holland that he was now working in Switzerland.

Mr. Chew Hong, or Chew Tong—he is known by both names—was called for a corollary purpose, to establish the identity of the New China Daily News, which figured in the testimony of Mr. Lattimore and some of the other witnesses. Now, we tried to reach him, and apparently he has left the country. The marshal reported that he cannot be found anywhere.

And again, on all of these, we have asked the Department of Justice to help us.

Again, Chew Hong, from the best information we have, is also in Red China.

Now, Anthony Jenkinson we had an address for at 133 West Forty-fourth Street, New York. We got some information that he might be found through the Allied Labor News at 401 Broadway. A subpena was issued at both of those places, and the marshal reported that he could not be found. We do know that he is an Englishman, and then we have every reason to believe that he has left the United States and is now in England.

Hans Mueller, who was known as Asiaticus, to the best of our knowledge, has died. All of the Institute of Pacific Relations people, and Holland and Carter, have stated that their best information is that he was killed during the last war. We have made no other efforts to try to reach him. He is not an American citizen.

Fred Poland is a Canadian, and we made no effort to reach him, because he is a Canadian official.

Now, we tried to reach Hilda Austern Rae, and we subpenaed her on March 11, 1952, and we got a report from the marshal's office that she was in Geneva, Switzerland, at that time.

Ludwig Rajchman, whose name appeared in our testimony, is now associated with the Polish Communist delegation to the United Nations and presumably would not be a witness before this Committee.

Andrew Roth, according to our evidence, according to information received from Mr. Holland, was last discovered to be in London. We have further evidence that the French Government has banned Mr. Roth from turning up in Indochina, because of his hostility to the French Government. I suppose vis-à-vis their difficulty with the Communists in Indochina.

Agnes Smedley is deceased. According to all reports, she is dead.

Andrew Steiger, who has appeared in our hearings particularly in connection with having written a book for Mr. Wallace—we had an address for him at 49 Claremont Avenue, in New York City. William Holland gave us the same information. We had a subpena out quite some time trying to reach Mr. Steiger, and it was all unavailing.

The last we heard from Guenther Stein was that he was believed to be a correspondent for the Hindustani Times in Geneva. Mr. Holland confirmed this fact. Several times in the course of the hearings we had testimony to the effect that he had been deported from France for espionage activities, but he has not been found by the committee, and we are not going to call him.

Anna Louise Strong we tried to subpena. We had an address for her in Connecticut, and after we tried to subpena her we discovered

Appendix VI—"Funfergruppen"

The following two articles by Simeyon Rostovsky, writing under the pseudonym Ernst Henri, were published in August 1933 in the New Statesman and Nation, *a British periodical for left-wing intellectuals.*

Although relating to Germany, the articles were an invitation to the magazine's readers to copy the Germans and form secret, subversive five-man communist "cells." Rostovsky/Henri was subtly following up Reilly's view that the Soviets should not confine their recruiting activities in Britain to the working classes but concentrate on gaining secret adherents from among those members of the "establishment" who were politically inclined to the left.

THE REVOLUTIONARY MOVEMENT IN NAZI GERMANY

(1) THE GROUPS OF FIVE (" FÜNFERGRUPPEN ")

[*This article, based on intimate knowledge of the situation in Germany, throws light on a movement whose activities are known to few foreigners and probably to only a minority of Germans. The facts as set out by the writer are, we believe, not open to question; the opinions expressed are his own. Next-week we hope to publish a second article by Mr. Henri on the revolutionary press in Germany.*—ED., *N.S. & N.*]

Is there still a Germany to-day apart from Hitler? It appears to be unthinkable. The news which comes from Germany daily speaks of a sudden transformation of an entire nation—of the end of all parties, of the disappearance of all non-National Socialist organisations and leaders, of the cessation of all non-Fascist thought. There is nothing outside Hitler. That is the truth, but it is only half the truth. The other half is the existence of a new subterranean revolutionary Germany.

There is perhaps no other example in history of a secret revolutionary movement with a completely equipped organisa-

tion and an effective influence extending over the whole country,
being able to develop in so short a time. Practically every
one of the larger factories contains a secret revolutionary
group ; in almost every district in the larger towns illegal
organisations and printing-presses are at work ; almost every
day in Berlin, Hamburg, Essen, Leipzig and other industrial
cities, anti-Fascist hand-bills, leaflets and posters appear in
the streets, local strikes break out in all directions ; and the
feelers of this organisation are manifestly stretching right into
the cohorts of the Nazi Storm Troops. This entire movement
has come into existence in within three or four months of
Hitler's *coup d'état*. And it will be stronger than any of its
forerunners. It has little of the romance of the old revolutionary
movements, of the Russian anti-Tsarists, of the Spanish Republicans, of the Italian insurgents. It has nothing of the
nationalist pathos or of the religious poeticism of the youngest
of the world's revolutionary movements—of the Irish Free
Staters; of the Indian Swarajists, of the Macedonian terrorists.
Its characteristic is that of a sober minded, scientific organisation of struggle and conspiracy and a military mass formation,
which lays hold not of small individual groups, but of an
entire social class. This organisation, which socially and
politically is not based only upon the thirteen million former
Socialist and Communist electors in Germany, is to-day dogging
Hitler's every footstep. In a few months time it may become
more dangerous for him than all the old parliamentary opposition
parties which he has hurled with such ease into the abyss.

Its core lies in the so-called *revolutionary groups of five*, a
novel form of anti-Fascist organisation, which, under Communist
leadership, has taken the place of the former party unions and
associations. These groups of five cover practically the whole
of German industry ; almost all the factories and the majority
of the more important offices are honeycombed with them.
Each group comprises approximately five persons, who as
far as possible are employed in the same section, industrial
and office workers, who formerly belonged to bodies of varied
political complexions—to the Social Democratic Trade Unions,
to the Reichsbanner, to the Christian Societies, to the Com-
munistic R.G.O. (Red Trade Union Opposition)—or even
were quite unorganised and politically indifferent. Together
these persons form a small, compact, secret brotherhood,
who in their hatred of the Hitler dictatorship and in defence
against Nazi terror have become completely amalgamated,

have buried all previous differences and pursue only one policy
—anti-Fascism. Because each group of this kind is limited to
just a few persons, it is almost invisible from outside and almost
unseizable ; how can one follow up and control conversations
and meetings of four or five persons during a rest interval
inside a factory, in a private house during a radio performance,
or on an excursion into the woods on a Sunday ? In the
larger workshops there are dozens of such groups of five, which
work independently of each other as far as possible and often
are not mutually acquainted. Should a group be discovered
and arrested (or ejected from the shop) the others carry on.
But they are co-ordinated from above ; the leadership and
central direction of all the groups of five in a town or in a local
industrial establishment are in the hands of a higher authority,
of a narrower and more exclusive conspiratorial organisation,
the " sub-district committee," consisting of a few experienced
revolutionaries. The contact between this local centre and the
workshops is generally maintained by one individual, the
revolutionary " workshop inspector," who holds the threads
of all the groups of five in one single workshop. This works
inspector has the most responsible and the most dangerous
post in the entire anti-Fascist organisation, for he knows
both the staff in the workshops and the secret addresses of
the local centres. The whole attention of the Hitler police,
and of the factory management which the Nazis appoint, is
mainly directed to the discovery of these people. But that
only happens in the rarest cases, and the anti-Fascist fighting
spirit is so strong in the German factories that reinforcements
and substitutes are always to be found—frequently from the
ranks of those who used not to be in the least interested in
political affairs. The whole of this secret machinery, startling
as it may seem to English readers, is in fact now the sole
practical form in which the political thought and will of millions
of men who have been reduced to silence in Hitler's " Totalitarian State " can realise itself. The purpose of the groups
of five is to revolutionise whole workshops, whole groups of
industrial and office workers, and to undermine the new
economic organisation of the Hitler State, which, like Mussolini's
prototype, must be founded on the Fascist corporations of
the workers, of the so-called " National Socialist Workshop
Organisation." (N.S.B.O.). The Nazis, who have suspended
all Trade Unions and independent labour bodies, are endeavouring by means of coercion and propaganda to force all the workers

into their N.S.B.O. organisation, where under the command
of Nazi leaders they will become the second line of the " Totalitarian State," of which the Storm Troops and the S.S. form
the first line. And the revolutionary groups of five are in
fact nothing else than the opposite poles of these State organisations of the Nazis in the factories. They constitute a
serious danger to the entire Hitler experiment of the " corporate
State," for their work consists not merely in bringing together
and holding together the elements which were already anti-
Fascist, but also in leading an offensive for the moral capture
of the remaining workers, even those who have accepted the
National Socialist regime.

The groups of five flood the factories with anti-Fascist propaganda material which they receive from the local anti-
Fascist centres. Even the Fascist newspapers in Germany
have lately mentioned this " pest " and have demanded
" Draconian counter-measures." Revolutionary factory newspapers (little handwritten or typewritten sheets, which are
published for a single workshop), handbills, leaflets, small
paper strips with a few fighting slogans or bits of news are
stuck up daily in the factories, pasted on the walls, on the
machinery, in the lavatories, on the doors of the worker's
home before he leaves in the morning. The whole fronts
of houses in the working class areas are covered with revolutionary slogans in paint which is difficult to wash off. The Nazis
have caught dozens of people, especially youths, at this job and
have sent them to concentration camps or penitentiaries
(the average punishment for such acts or for distributing
revolutionary literature in connection with this has been raised
during the past few weeks from six months to eighteen months
imprisonment) ; but the walls of the houses and the fences
still continue their protest against Hitlerism. In this way it
has been possible to revive courage and give a fresh assurance to
the masses of the workers who in the first days of the revolution
and the terror seemed to be paralysed by fright. But still
more important is the other effect of the groups of five. The
whole official Trade Union leadership in the factories, the
settlement of wage rates, relationship with the employers and
so on, are to-day in the hands of the National Socialist Workshop Organisation (N.S.B.O.). In most cases the entire staff
is simply forced to come into the N.S.B.O. by the summoning
of a detachment of armed Storm Troops or by the threat of

instant dismissal. But at the same time there enters the revolutionary group of five, which often immediately becomes the most active element inside the N.S.B.O. They begin " in the, name of National Socialism " by urging the N.S.B.O. to put forward a demand for an increase of wages—for before his victory Hitler promised higher wages for all workers. They force the N.S.B.O. always, in the name and under the protection of the former Nazi programme, to demand the fulfilment of the old demagogic promises, shorter working-hours, improved working conditions, and the removal of unpopular directors or officials. The result is that in the last few weeks the first wave of strikes since Hitler's victory has broken over Germany (though strikes are forbidden in the Hitler State), that in numerous cases the management in Nazi factories has been compelled officially to " postpone " the intended wage-reductions for two months, that the Nazi " Reichs Association of Industrial Employers " addressed a protest to the Chancellor against the attitude of the N.S.B.O. and that Hitler has come into conflict with a large number of his own local N.S.B.O. organisations, and indeed has been obliged to dissolve some of them for being " tainted with Marxism."

Thus the revolutionary groups of five who are concealed inside the Fascist N.S.B.O. achieve a twofold result ; they disorganise the National Socialist economic and party apparatus, and they dispel the illusion spread among the masses of the workers by Nazi demagogy.   ERNST HENRI

IN GERMANY.—II

THE REVOLUTIONARY PRESS AND AGITATION*

THOUGH the groups of five form only part of the revolutionary movement in Nazi Germany, they are certainly the most important part—the mass basis of the movement. As a working-class organisation its main sphere of activity is in the factories and offices, where the real roots of any such movement must be. It is from this source that a future revolution against the Hitler Dictatorship must start. But in addition to this secret revolutionary movement there is also developing a political propaganda which is directed, as the propaganda of the old political parties used to be, towards the general public.

There is to-day an extensive revolutionary press and a broad revolutionary agitation in Germany, which is uniting itself with the groups of five. If these latter represent the soldiers of the revolutionary movement, the mass reserves in the factories, one further step up the ladder we find the organisation of the revolutionary officers, the staffs of the revolutionary movement in Germany. This is a much closer and more specialised organisation, which is in the main identical with the old inner apparatus of the Communists—the only organisation which has survived the establishment of the Third Reich of Hakenkreuzlers. We will refer later to the special rôle of the Communists. But the scope of the new revolutionary press in Germany, which is already distributing every day hundreds of thousands of papers, and which already represents a real power, has to-day grown far beyond the framework of that party. Around this and taking part in its distribution are gathering to-day thousands of former Social Democrats and Reichsbanner men, non-party people, Jews and even former Liberals and Catholics—all that is still actively anti-Fascist and hates Hitler and his terror State. It is a political and journalistic revolution. The German revolutionary of to-day is first of all a technical artist, a conspiratorial genius and frequently a magician. His editorial office is any little room, which often has to be changed daily and frequently more than once in a day. He enters it and leaves it at the peril of his life, or else he lives, eats, and sleeps, confined in it. His printing press is only seldom a proper machine workshop, it is generally a duplicator, a typewriter, very often just a simple shilling ink blotter, on which a strip of linoleum with words carved on it are stuck. A blotter of this kind produces in a night hundreds of small handbills! At the beginning of July the Hitler police discovered in the neighbourhood of Neumünster, in Schleswig Holstein, a revolutionary printing press in a cavity 2½ metres deep. Some 300,000 copies of the weekly edition of the Communist *Rote Fahne* are issued. This centrally printed edition is reproduced throughout Germany by local groups of from five to thirty men working with duplicators, typewriters, and by hand. The fly-leaves and handbills with a few, generally five

to ten, lines of anti-Fascist slogans and revelations
are innumerable. All this is reminiscent of the secret
revolutionary press of the Germany of 1848. But to-day
the language used is short, sharp, and practical. Long-drawn
idealist meditations are not to be found. Who are the authors ?
An illegal paper of the Communist revolutionaries, *Freiheit*,
supplies the answer : " Editor—Karl Marx."

More important than the printing are the distribution and
circulation of this press inside German towns which are
swarming with armed and suspicious Storm Troops. For
these purposes a special art and science have been
recreated to meet the new conditions. The streets, the underground railways, the restaurants, the parks, the unemployment
exchanges are often full of this literature ; it is in the hands
of the passers by ; it gets into private houses. The Nazis
themselves admit this in their daily police appeals against the
burrowing of the " red sub-humans."

But how is this managed without the entire organisation
being discovered in a couple of days ? Here, too, the revolutionaries work according to the same principle as the groups
of five in the workshops : the organisation is so divided that
one man does not know another. The different distributors
and sellers of the newspapers and leaflets have their particular
collection stations, but they do not know who brings the newspapers there ; if such a distributor be caught, the police car
hardly find out anything from him. Still less can the
police run after all the children who find ingenious
ways of distributing anti-Fascist propaganda and messages
in the streets. Nor can anyone know that anti-Fascist
literature is being sent in the official postal envelopes
of various authorities ; not long ago in Berlin the police
discovered that the Post Office had for weeks been trans-
mitting, at the expense of the State, revolutionary matter in
envelopes which bore the imprint of the head office of the
city electricity works, and which had been requisitioned by
the anti-Fascists. On June 24th the police discovered a
large " astrological " business in Heinestrasse in Berlin, where
15,000 " horoscopes " were all ready for despatch—all revolutionary appeals. There are hundreds of methods of this sort,
and the German revolutionaries invent new ones every day. A
good deal of this literature is masked outside in the most careful
manner. A few weeks ago a sixteen-page film advertisement,

first few pages of the leaflet chatted amiably about Nero and
ancient Rome, but then suddenly jumped to the burning of the
Reichstag, and revealed Hitler, Göring and Goebbels as the
real incendiaries. A second pamphlet against Hitler is called
Art and Knowledge, and in Bavaria a revolutionary leaflet
has spread over the entire page the large title : " Newest
Sensation !   The latest cheap wireless set !   Four Years
guarantee. You must have our radio." But the small text
in between is propaganda against the Nazi Government.
The so-called revolutionary " chain-letters " have become a
real " plague." Somebody gets a political anti-Fascist letter
with the demand to copy it several times and to send
it with the same instructions to his friends. Entire quarters
of Berlin are writing these " letters."

They cannot kill the press of the people—this is proved
once again in Nazi Germany. These leaflets are often
technically very imperfect, even almost unreadable. But who
worries about that at present in Germany ? The same could
be said of the leaflets of the French Revolution, of those issued
by the fighters of 1848, and by the Russian revolutionaries :
later on these became history. In a country where one is
only allowed to read, write and think as a National-Socialist,
illegal leaflets are snatched out of one's hand. This press is
a growing power.

The groups of five and the illegal press are the two chief
weapons by which the revolutionary movement in Germany
is forcing its way from underground to the surface of the
totalitarian State and is undermining two of its pillars—
the economic apparatus and the monopoly of public opinion.
And perhaps the third and most important pillar of Hitler's
dictatorship will also soon be undermined—its military
apparatus. In many places in Germany inside the S.A.,
revolutionary organisations, " groups of revolutionary S.A.
men," as they are called, have come into existence. Some
of these even publish their own papers and distribute them
in the barracks. (On June 10th, in Dusseldorf, an S.A. man
of Standard 39 was shot for distributing such leaflets.) These
groups begin to exploit the growing disatisfaction of the S.A.
men about their economic position, the luxurious life of their
leaders, the non-fulfilment of earlier Socialist promises, the
refusal to allow them to join the ordinary police, etc. It seems

as if the growth of these secret S.A. organisations had had something to do with the great S.A. revolt which broke out in Germany at the end of June—the rebellion of the Frankfurt

S.A., the dissolution of the famous Horst Wessel detachment in Berlin, and of some formations in Dresden, and the great street demonstrations of S.A. men in Bochum and Kassel, where they sang the *International*. This movement, which is just at the beginning, should not be exaggerated. But it is quite evident that in the long run the S.A.—this mass of 800,000 mercenary soldiers, partly recruited from the proletariat, cannot possibly be satisfied by Hitler and · might become a new revolutionary explosive force. Hitler and Göring are already trying to protect themselves against it, by transferring police functions from the S.A. to the S.S. (Guard detachments), which are the much smaller and more devoted bodyguard of the Government. But this merely aggravates the uneasiness in the S.A. Again, in the labour-service camps, the new great massing points where, under the cloak of "manual education," military drill is really being forced upon hundreds of thousands of youths—here too revolutionary groups are at work.

Göring is trying to set up a terrifying organisation against the growing spectre of the new revolutionary movement— the newly formed "Secret State police force" (Geheimes Staatspolizei-Amt, or the G.S.P.)—a grandiose spy and terror organisation. It is to combine the old methods of the Russian Ochrana with the new experiences of the secret agency of Mussolini, and to form an unprecedented synthesis of police science. This organisation, unlimited money and men at its disposal, has only one task—to catch revolutionaries. Its real spiritual inspirer is Goebbels, and its centre is the same secret circle of Nazi-terrorists who organised the Reichstag fire. This organisation works day and night, its agents are spread throughout the country, and it works by torture of prisoners and suspects. But how far can the secret State police with all its spies, instruments of torture and vast organisation succeed against the heroism, the courage and indomitable inventive genius of these people? What can the secret State police do against the new system of demonstration of the revolutionaries, the "lightning demonstrations," where several hundred people suddenly appear in a certain place, at a certain signal, from side streets, shout anti-Hitler slogans, distribute leaflets, and then, in a few minutes, disappear again among the passers-by ? What can the secret State police do against the new meeting system of the revolutionaries, where small groups of harmless hikers—linked up by couriers and protected by sentries—meet in a wood, couples evidently very much in love !

What indeed can any secret police do against a revolutionary movement springing from the people ? ERNST HENRI

Appendix VII

The Lists of Members of Trinity College, Cambridge, published in April 1933 and April 1936, show up the names of Blunt, Burgess, Greenberg, Straight, and Long.

Complete List of Members of the University in Residence, With their Addresses;

Also a

List of Royal Engineers & Royal Air Force.

[*We issue this list at the beginning of each Term. It is requested that all corrections and alterations of address may be made known to the Printers, at the Office, in Corn Exchange Street. Our thanks are due to all those whose assistance has enabled us to issue this List.*]

Cambridge Review Extra Number

April 22, 1933

TRINITY.

M.A., &c.

Bevan, Professor A. A., G, Whewell's court
Bidder, G. P., Sc.D., Cavendish corner,
   Hills road 502
Bidwell, J. E., 2, King's Parade and Fox
   hill, Great Shelford 12
Bingham, Rev. C. R., Great Shelford
Black, M., L 2, Nevile's court 580
Blunt, A. F., A 2, The Bishop's Hostel 580
Boughey, Rev. A. H. F., 4, Cranmer road
   267

3rd Year.

Bosanquet, S. J. A., G 5, Whewell's court
Brocklebank, G. R., 27, Park parade
Brooke, J. W., A 5, The Bishop's Hostel
Burgess. G. F. de M., I 4, New court
Burridge, L. M., C 1, New court
Burroughes, J. H. L., K 5, New court
Butler, P. J., 9, Portugal street

April 23, 1936

TRINITY.

M.A., &c.

Besicovitch, A. S., F.R.S., E, Great court
Bidder, G. P., Sc.D., Cavendish corner, Hills road 87502
Bidwell, J. E., 2, King's parade and Fox hill, Great Shelford 12
Black, M., The King's Hostel 3441
Blunt, A. F., C 2, Nevile's court 3441
Bosworth, R. C. L., Ph.D. 57, Roseford rd
Boughey, Rev. A. H. F., 4, Cranmer road 4632

3rd Year.

Gell, P. G. H., A 2, The Bishop's Hostel
Gibson, M. O. J., I 10, New court
Gibson, W. D., K 9, Whewell's court
Goodwyn, P. A., G 4, New court
Grant, J. A., A 1, New court
Grant, M., A 4, The Bishop's Hostel
Greenberg, M., B 7, New court
Greenwell, P. McC., R 5, Great court
Grimsey, A. H. R., I 4, New court

2nd Year.

Stanhope-Lovell, W. B., 25, Park parade
Stevens, J. E., 9, Jesus lane
Stewart, R. H., 17, Chesterton road
Stewart, W., 8, Jesus lane
Straight, M. W., K 5, Whewell's court
Studt, W. H., 155, Chesterton road
Syrett, J. D. A., 20, Jesus lane

1st Year.

Leacock, J. T., 11, Portugal street
Lewin, H. G. D., 60, Maid's causeway
Little, T. D., 36, Sidney street
Llewellyn, D. T., 5, St Mary's passage
Long, L. H., A 7, New court
Longman, M. F. K., 8, Malcolm street
Longman, T. M. 36, Sidney street

Notes

CHAPTER I

1. Chrezvychainaya Komisseya (Extraordinary Commission for Combatting Counter-Revolution, Sabotage, and Speculation). The Bolshevik successor organization to the Tsarist Police, the Okhrana.
2. Those arrested included the American Kalamatiano. In *Reilly: Ace of Spies*, I incorrectly wrote that he had been executed along with the other conspirators who had been arrested. In fact, although condemned to death, after strong pressure from the U.S. government he was eventually released in 1921.
3. In 1984, a Russian film crew, engaged in making a film of the history of Soviet Russia from 1918 to 1946, flew in from Moscow to interview me in London about Reilly— and brought me a very nice bottle of vodka into the bargain! The director claimed to have seen the house in Odessa where Reilly was born and stated that there was a Rosenblum relative who still lived next door.
4. Richard Deacon is the author of *History of the British Secret Service, History of the Japanese Secret Service, The Cambridge Apostles*, and many other books.
5. Sorge was arrested by the Japanese in 1941. Disowned by Stalin, he was hanged. Only in 1964 was this brilliant Soviet agent, who sent Stalin prior advice of Japan's intention to enter the war, honored posthumously. He was made a Hero of the Soviet Union, a street was named after him and even postage stamps were issued with Sorge's picture.
6. St. Anthony's College, Oxford, holds quite extensive pa-

pers on Colonel Akashi ("Colonel Akashi and Japanese contacts with Russian Revolutionaries 1904–1905").

7. MI1C officially became the SIS (Secret Intelligence Service) in 1921 and was later also known as MI6.

8. Boris Savinkov, leading Social Revolutionary and Minister of War in the Kerensky Government of 1917. Prominent anti-Bolshevik in the 1920s.

9. The Cheka was renamed the Gosudarstvennoye Politicheskoye Upravlyenive in 1922 (State Security for Combatting Counter-Revolution).

10. Kontrarazvedyvatelni Otdel (Counterespionage Department).

11. An English translation of this letter, not previously published, is included in Appendix II.

12. Komitet Gosudarstvennoy Bezopasnoti (Committee for State Security).

13. C.f. the mysteries surrounding the death of Jan Masaryk and, more recently, that of the British Midland Bank's man in Moscow, Dennis Skinner, soon after MI5 traitor Bettaney attempted to defect in 1984. Both Masaryk and Skinner "fell" out of windows.

14. Joseph Climens Pilsudski (1803–1935), President of Poland, 1916–1926, Prime Minister, 1926–1928, and Minister of War, 1926–1928.

15. "Dezinformatsia" or "Aktivnyye Meroprivatiya" covers the whole gamut of Soviet overt and covert techniques for influencing ideas and events in foreign countries.

16. Narodny Kommissariat knutrennyich Del. The new name given by Stalin in 1934 to the GPU.

CHAPTER II

1. The late British diplomat Reginald Bridgeman, who knew Reilly well, wrote to the British author Richard Deacon: "To me Reilly always admitted that in the long run it might be better to join them than to fight them."

2. In particular those of Vladislav Minaev and Lev Nikulin, the Soviet quasi-authoritative historians of Soviet counterespionage.

3. Melor stands for Marx, Engels, October Revolution: a name given not infrequently to their sons by ardent communists in the 1920s.

4. *Professional Anticommunism*, by Ernst Henri, Moscow, 1981. A chapter on Sidney Reilly describes him as a "terrorist" but makes no mention whatsoever of his demise.

5. "Kak ya iskal shpiona Reili" (1968).

6. See note 2, above.

7. "Lockhart Plot or Dzerzhinsky Plot," by Richard K. Debo. (*Journal of Modern History*, Vol. XLIII, 1971.) (The Late De Witt C. Poole, American Consul-General in Moscow in 1918, was also of the opinion that Reilly was an agent-provocateur of Dzerzhinsky.)

8. Lenin's mother was half Jewish.

CHAPTER III

1. Rear Admiral Sir Manfield Cumming retired at the beginning of 1923 because of ill-health and died a few months later. His successor, Admiral Sinclair, was a former Director of Naval Intelligence.

2. In a bizarre coincidence Toivo Vjahi also "died" a traitor's death soon afterward: an excellent cover revealed only when he surfaced forty years later as KGB Colonel I. M. Petrov. (*Pravda*, November 26th, 1967, "A Man and His Name—The Story of a Soviet Intelligence Officer.")

3. Books and articles by Amadtsky, Golinkov, Kremlev, Nikulin Minaev, Pogoda, and other Soviet writers.

CHAPTER IV

1. Inostannyi Otdel, the GPU's Foreign Department.

2. Trilisser and Artuzov were both liquidated later by Stalin.

3. In *Reilly: Ace of Spies*, I described Dagmara as being the niece of one of Reilly's great friends, the lawyer Alexander Grammatikov. The same Soviet source claims that Dagmara was his daughter.

4. With the exception of Trotsky, for whose assassination he was responsible, all Stalin's fellow coffin bearers were later executed following "show trials." Lubianka Square

has been renamed Dzerzhinsky Square, and there a statue of Dzerzhinsky is also to be found. In its sedateness the square still retains much of its character of pre-revolutionary times, despite its subsequent heavy involvement in murder, torture, and bloodshed.

CHAPTER V

1. See Chapters 8 and 9.
2. See Chapter 10.

CHAPTER VI

1. His personal driver, and friend, in Poland was one May Besonov, who later became Stalin's chauffeur.
2. Arrested in 1937 during Stalin's purges and probably died in an "isolator"—an NKVD prison where political prisoners were kept incommunicado for life.
3. The archetypes of those who today machine-gun anyone caught trying to escape across the Iron Curtain from the East to the freedom of the West.
4. A term used to describe the head of Soviet intelligence in the country or area concerned. The body of GPU officers working directly under the rezident were known as the "rezidentura."
5. These delegations have always "traded" more in secrets than in commerce and business.
6. "Cells" of five.
7. Rutherford, a Nobel prize winner, made a peer for his services to science, disapproved of the massive expenditure entailed in large-scale atom splitting. He died in 1937 and would have been horrified by the atom bomb.
8. On his return to Russia, Kapitsa was made Director of the Institute of Physical Problems at the Academy of Sciences. He was dismissed in 1946 and put under house arrest for refusing to work on nuclear weapons but reinstated after Stalin's death in 1953. His work made possible the launching of the first two Sputniks. He died in 1984. Today, Russian scientists live under better material conditions than

most, have freedom in their work, but in no circumstances may they become involved in politics.

9. Yagoda was sacked by Stalin for "slackness" and following arrest and participation in a show trial in 1937, was shot.

10. One of the most detailed accounts of Stalin's brutality and of the purge trials is to be found in the Russian historian Roy Medvedev's book *Let History Judge* (Alfred A. Knopf, New York, 1971).

11. The letter was taken to France by an American cousin of Orlov's and delivered to the Soviet Embassy in Paris.

12. Yezhov was replaced the same year by Lavrenty Pavlovich Beria and disappeared soon after. In 1956 Khrushchev revealed in a secret report to the Twentieth Party Congress that Yezhov had been a degenerate and had paid for his crimes.

CHAPTER VII

1. Underground cells or "rings" of five. Arthur Koestler was one of those who joined a Ring of Five in Germany at about this time. Later he was to write: "I went to communism as one goes to a spring of fresh water and I left communism as one clambers out of a poisoned river stream with the wreckage of flooded cities and the corpses of the drowned." (See Appendix IV.)

2. Russian Telegraph Agency.

3. Telegrafnoye Agentstvo Sovietskogo Soyuza.

4. Opened in April 1924 with Christov Roskovsky as Chargé d'Affaires in small offices at 128 New Bond Street. His staff of three included a naval attaché.

5. The Agitation and Propaganda Department of the party's Central Committee.

6. The exact date of Rostovsky's arrival in Britain is not known but it was probably in 1932.

7. The GPU/NKVD *rezident* in Britain in the 1930s was the Russian Samuel Cahan.

8. Incredibly, Howard and Blunt were later recruited by MI5.

9. The "cells of five" idea originated during the nineteenth century and was adopted by French, Austrian, and other

revolutionaries. They have come into use again in the
1980s in Poland to oppose communism. They are termed
KOS (Circles of Social Resistance); and again, each "Circle" consists of only five people.

10. Both Reilly's close colleague, the late Brigadier George
Hill, and the late Eleanor Toye, a onetime SI5 agent and
Reilly's secretary and mistress, voiced their opinion to me
that Reilly was bisexual. Eleanor Toye confided to me that
Reilly was not a great lover: "He was the kind of man
who would make love while reading *The Financial Times*
on the pillow."

11. Michael Straight's book contains a group photograph of
some members of the Cambridge Union which includes
Pieter Keuneman, Maurice Dobb, Michael Straight himself, and Leo Long, who confessed in 1964 to being a
Soviet agent.

12. From Graham Greene's introduction to Kim Philby's *My
Silent War* (McGibbon & Kee, 1968).

13. *My Silent War* (Grove Press, New York, 1968).

14. One former member of the British Communist Party who
worked closely with Rostovsky during the war still recalls
the "thrill of it" when reading the Ernst Henri "funfergruppen" articles as a young man. Only some fifty years
later did he come to learn that Rostovsky and Henri were
the same person!

15. There is a school of thought that the Zinoviev letter, published *after* Savinkov had returned to Russia and *after* the
presumed time of Reilly's decision to switch his loyalty
over to Moscow, was genuine. The theory is that Reilly
deliberately raised suspicions that he had been responsible
for the forging in order to exonerate the Soviet Union, his
new mistress-to-be.

CHAPTER VIII

1. Another claim she made in later life was to have been a
pre–World War I graduate of Cambridge, although the
university did not admit women before 1914. It is believed

that she spent a few months studying English at Newnham, then a college for girls.

2. Nina Berberova, a well-known Russian émigré writer and academic, lives in the United States. Her biography, *Zheleznaya Zhenchina (The Iron Woman)*, after a nickname Gorki gave to Moura, is at present available only in Russian, published in the United States by Russica Publishing in 1981. She and her husband, on legitimate Soviet passports, lived as guests of Gorki in his house in Italy from 1922 to 1925, when Moura was his constant companion.

3. Peters, who like Litvinov had an English wife, along with other former Dzerzhinsky aides was executed on Stalin's orders in 1930 by those who replaced them. Subsequently the new men were shot by other new men.

4. Moura once told me that she had been temporarily imprisoned in 1918 in the same cell as eight women, all of whom, on interrogation, claimed to be Reilly's wife.

5. Gorki had an adopted son in the French Foreign Legion who went by the name of Zinovy Pieshkov. His real name was Sverdlov, brother of Yakov Sverdlov (1858–1919), Chairman of the Soviet Central Executive Committee and, during 1918–1919, Lenin's closest collaborator.

6. Smuggled out of Russia in the Swedish diplomatic bags, some sixty letters written by Moura to my father during this period came into my possession on my father's death. They make fascinating reading but unfortunately the family has refused to allow me to publish any of them.

7. H. G. Wells, *Experiment in Autobiography*, Victor Gollancz (1934) and reissued by Faber & Faber (1984). A translation approved by Wells of the quite lengthy discussion he had with Stalin included the following statement he made to Stalin: "My visit to the United States excited my mind. The old-fashioned world is collapsing."

8. It is not clear where they met. Undoubtedly the Baroness would not have admitted that this had been in the Soviet Union.

CHAPTER IX

1. In the course of his career, Hill was awarded the D.S.O., the O.B.E. and the M.C.
2. Special Operations Executive, responsible for organizing resistance and sabotage behind enemy lines.
3. The code name for the German invasion of Russia.
4. In fact, Hill by now held the rank of Colonel. (He ended the war as Brigadier.)
5. The idea of a Western intelligence officer being appointed today as a liaison officer with the KGB is quite unthinkable!
6. The Soviet Foreign Ministry.
7. The manuscript of which is in my possession.

CHAPTER X

1. Winston S. Churchill, *The Second World War*, Vol. 5 (*Germany Drives East*).
2. Schulenburg was executed in November 1944 for involvement in the July 1944 attempt on Hitler's life.
3. Repressiya—the punishment of enemies of the state. Today the execution chambers have been largely replaced by so-called mental hospitals where political prisoners are given special drugs to destroy sleep and the nervous system. These drugs are the successors of Obezvolivaivshii, a drug given to prisoners to take away their will, leading to false confessions at trials.
4. During the expansion of the KGB in the 1970s the cells of the Lubianka were turned into offices. The main KGB prison is now the Lefortovo.
5. Lavrenty Pavlovich Beria, head of the NKVD (1938–1945). He liquidated his predecessor, Yezhov, who had reigned during the worst of Stalin's purges. Yezhov's predecessor, the butcher Yagoda, was also shot.
6. Ivan Ivanovich Maslennikov, Chief of Directorate of Border Guards (1938–1942) and a Deputy Chairman of the NKVD. Nikolay Ivanovich Yatsenko, Deputy Chief of Border Guards (1941–1945).
7. Vasiliy Vasilyevich Chernyshov, Head of Military section

of SMERSH (1942–1943) and Deputy Chief of the NKVD until 1952.

8. For a description of Beria's office, I am indebted to the late Brigadier George Hill, almost certainly the first Englishman and—"moles" apart—probably the only one to enter the office of the Head of the Soviet State Security.

9. Also in 1941, my father's name was put forward for the post of head of Britain's Secret Intelligence Service. In his diary he wrote: "Nothing on earth would induce me to accept—even if begged to take it." (He spent most of the war as Political Warfare Chief, which included the direction of both overt, or "white," and covert, or "black," propaganda.)

10. Amazingly, Goebbels' propaganda machine not infrequently also declared my father to be an arch-enemy who was destined for liquidation when Germany had won the war.

CHAPTER XI

1. It was in Cleveland that Orlov, after studying English at the Dyke and Spencerian College, spent a year writing his articles on Stalin in preparation for the day when he could feel free to publish them.

2. The Orlovs' daughter, Vera, who had never been in good health, died in 1939.

3. Orlov testified that Vasili Zubelin, second secretary at the Soviet Embassy during World War II, was "one of the outstanding operatives of the NKVD."

4. Former CIA Director General Walter Bedell Smith, in a statement to a Congressional committee, said: "I believe the communists are so activist and adept that they have infiltrated practically every security agency of the Government."

5. Glavnoye Razvedyvatelnoye Upravleniye (Soviet Military Intelligence). It operated quite separately from the NKVD, as it still does today from the KGB.

6. The General's estate was shared by several American cousins of Orlov.

CHAPTER XII

1. V. S. Abakumov, Chairman of the MGB (1951–1953) and former chief of SMERSH (an abbreviation of Smert Slpionem—Death to Spies). There are many who think SMERSH to be a fictional organization invented by Ian Fleming for his James Bond books. This is not so.
2. The MGB became the MVD in 1953, which in turn became the KGB in March 1954. The first head of the KGB was the abominable Ivan Serov.
3. The dreaded Beria was arrested in the summer of 1953 by one of his subordinates, Major General Nikolski, head of the MVD's 7th Administration (in charge of arrests and interrogations), and shot.
4. He has attacked both the British and the French Socialist parties for not being sufficiently left and also the Chinese for not following the Moscow line.
5. The methods used by Soviet agents to recruit, manipulate, and blackmail journalists of foreign nationality is another story altogether and one, because of the inevitable libel risks, virtually impossible to print.
6. *Soviet Directory of Multinational Publications in the Soviet Union*, Moscow (1985). This could equally well describe the objectives of TASS.
7. Sturua went on to become the *Izvestia* correspondent in Washington, where he was described to me by someone in the intelligence world as being "a real bad apple." Currently he is working in Moscow on matters relating to Third World countries, Communism's most fruitful field.

CHAPTER XIII

1. Reilly returned to Russia in 1925. To the best of my knowledge, Moura never came to England until 1929.
2. I do not recall the exact year, but it must have been in the period 1964–1967.

CHAPTER XIV

1. Czechoslovak Foreign Minister from 1965 until his mysterious death in March 1968.
2. Despite FBI warnings of his Soviet links, President Truman

persisted in his decision to appoint White to the International Monetary Fund. White was Assistant Secretary at the U.S. Treasury, and the spy-ring leader Elizabeth Bentley was later to declare that he was "one of our best avenues" for placing Communists in Government posts.

3. Elizabeth Bentley subsequently wrote a book, *Out of Bondage*, published in 1951 (Devin-Adair, New York).

4. Today, in the average Soviet Embassy, there are always a number of "open" KGB officers who are known to the Ambassador; these are occupied with security matters in safe, classified documents. The "covert" KGB Embassy staff will be unknown to the Ambassador and may number anywhere between five and ten people of varying ranks. (The head of the KGB *rezidentura* in any country may have been a "sleeper" for several years before being activated.)

5. To be published by Random House.

6. *FBI–KGB War*, by Robert Lamphere, Random House (1985).

7. At one period Philby, Burgess, and Maclean were all in Washington together. At the time of their defection both Burgess and Maclean had been drinking heavily and so was Philby. A theory exists that Philby had planned to defect at the same time as the other two men but at the last minute was ordered by the Soviets to remain *in situ*.

8. Maclean's ashes were brought back to Britain; Blunt died in the same year. Burgess, who had recruited Blunt, died in 1963; his ashes were also sent back to Britain. Burgess and Blunt were both sons of clergymen.

9. President Truman was even accused in the U.S. Senate of promoting White while knowing he was a Soviet spy.

10. Having been "named" by the former spy Whittaker Chambers, Lauchlin Currie fled to South America to escape trial.

11. Maclean and Allan Nunn May were both at Trinity Hall College.

12. This was also a name used in the U.S. by Gusev, who on occasion called himself "P. Green." The true identity of the Soviet agent "Michael Green" is still a "classified" matter.

13. In *After Long Silence*, Michael Straight refers to the pre-ponderance of homosexuals among Cambridge Commu-nists. During my own time at Cambridge, Kings College rather than Trinity was considered the "home" of homo-sexuals.

14. It is believed that Reilly, who had been responsible for the forgery of the "Zinoviev Letter" in the 1920s, may have been the schemer behind the multimillion-dollar counter-feit ring which flooded the United States with forged hundred-dollar bills in 1934.

15. Most people are unaware that the real author of the book was the British communist Cedric Belfrage, who sold his interest in the book to Albert Kahn and Michael Sayers. Belfrage eventually showed up in Moscow, according to Bogolepov, a Soviet Foreign Ministry defector.

16. These functions, as opposed to normal intelligence work, are known as *aktivnyye meropriyatiya* (Active Measures).

17. Okharanivoye Otdelyene. Today, the KGB still uses the word *Okhrana* to describe the 16,000 guards it employs to protect the Russian leaders, including its own hierarchy. Loosely speaking, the Okhrana guards are the Russian equivalent of U.S. Secret Service men.

18. *Les Russes sont arrivés*, Cyril Ghenkin, Scarabie & Cie, Paris (1984).

CHAPTER XV

1. The headquarters staff of MI6 had also been cut back to about the same number.

2. Major Alley had been born and brought up in Russia and had been head of the British Secret Service in Russia until April 1918, when he returned to London and subsequently transferred to MI5. I had occasion to meet him from time to time during World War II, when, like many intelligence officers, he was in uniform. He seemed to have as many medal ribbons on his chest as General MacArthur but I never learned what they were all for.

3. So called because of the "war" with gangsterdom.

4. The Communist Party of the United States merged with the Communist Labor Party in 1921; members pledged themselves "to defend the Soviet Union and to ensure the triumph of Soviet power in the United States."

5. Espionage abroad devolved later on the OSS, the forerunner of the CIA. The latter's function also came to include counterespionage abroad.

6. Liaison was established through the Inter-Agency Intelligence Committee, which was subsequently to include Air Force Intelligence.

7. Given that virtually every secret agency in the world has been penetrated at different times, it would not be altogether surprising if there were, or have been, some *unknown* cases of moles in the FBI.

8. The U.S. Immigration and Nationalization Service has an Intelligence Unit and an Anti-Subversive Unit and works in close liaison with the FBI.

9. The story of Colonel Rudolf Abel's trial and eventual exchange for Gary Powers is excellently told in *Strangers on a Bridge*, by James B. Donovan, Abel's defense lawyer (Atheneum, New York, 1964). Abel died in 1971, while Powers was killed in an air crash in 1977.

10. *Too Secret Too Long* (St. Martin's Press, New York, 1984). Hollis, incidentally, was not a Cambridge graduate. He was at Worcester College, Oxford.

11. A book by Lonsdale in English, *Spy: Twenty Years in Soviet Secret Service*, was published in 1965 (Hawthorn Blake, New York).

12. Government Communications Headquarters (the British cipher-breaking intelligence organization).

13. Ironically, the code name given to Sidney Reilly by the British Secret Intelligence Service was "ST1."

CHAPTER XVI

1. *Secrecy and Democracy: The CIA in Transition*, by Admiral Stansfield Turner, Houghton Mifflin (1985).

Index